GREYHOUND AT THE GRAVESITE

PETS REPORTER MYSTERY BOOK #1

KYLA COLBY

Cover Design by Stunning Book Covers

Edited by Margarita Martinez

For information and rights inquiries contact:

kylacolby.com

kyla@kylacolby.com

For the Keybangers

CONTENTS

Free Cozy Novella   vii

Prologue   1
Chapter 1   13
Chapter 2   24
Chapter 3   31
Chapter 4   39
Chapter 5   50
Chapter 6   59
Chapter 7   69
Chapter 8   79
Chapter 9   88
Chapter 10   100
Chapter 11   112
Chapter 12   120
Chapter 13   126
Chapter 14   139
Chapter 15   149
Chapter 16   155
Chapter 17   163
Chapter 18   172
Chapter 19   180
Chapter 20   188
Chapter 21   197
Chapter 22   201
Chapter 23   208
Chapter 24   214
About the Author   223

Please leave a review   225

PART I
PREVIEW: BOOK 2 BICHON FRISE NEAR
THE BODY

Chapter 1   229
Chapter 2   234
Chapter 3   244

Continue the series   255

Aplayful ukulele ringtone woke Sam Hodges from a deep sleep. She wished that whoever had invented the ringtone silencer for cell phones had also invented something to help her remember to activate it.

She checked the clock.

3:00.

Daylight streamed in through the windows of her childhood bedroom, so it must be 3 in the afternoon, not 3 a.m. Her eyes glanced from her debate team trophies, sitting proudly on a shelf, to a basket of pristine stuffed animals. The pink walls matched the carnations on her comforter, and stenciled cats ringed the ceiling molding. All the animals, of course, had been her mother's doing.

Sam grabbed her still-chiming phone off the night-stand. "Hello?"

"At approximately 12:15 p.m. on Sept. 3, a blue Honda sedan driven by Cathy Stilkington, 51, headed westbound, failed to stop at a stop sign at Orchard Road and Grand Canine Way, rolling through the intersection's crosswalk and striking Samantha Hodges, 26, on a gray bicycle."

The low, gruff voice was one Sam hadn't heard in years, but one she hadn't forgotten. She sat bolt upright. Frank Martin had been her first real boss when she'd interned at the *Birchwood Bugle* after college. Frank's reprimands early in her journalism career had stuck with her in a way later ones hadn't. Perhaps the later ones should have, Sam wished, realizing suddenly just why she was in her childhood bedroom, slinking back to her hometown with her tail between her legs after being fired—or something like it—from the *Chicago Times.*

"Hodges was taken to Parkview Medical Center and treated for a mild concussion. She was released at 1:30 p.m. in good health. Stilkington suffered no injuries and was given a $175 fine for failure to stop at an intersection. It is additionally noted that a man dressed as the Statue of Liberty, advertising outside of Jones' Family Accounting, rushed to help the injured and called police."

Though Frank continued reading, his voice low and rolling, it barely broke through Sam's reverie about her childhood in Birchwood, how destined she had been for success, and how horribly wrong things had gone after she'd landed her dream job.

"... Hodges?"

Frank Martin had been the first one to teach Sam the delicate art of silence—of waiting to ask another question, so that the interviewee felt compelled to fill the break in conversation and divulged more. She practiced that art now. But why, exactly, was Frank calling her about yesterday's accident?

"Saved by a Statue of Liberty, Hodges? And you didn't think to call your old editor with a news story tip like that?"

For the first time, Sam responded. Or tried to. She meant to say something coherent, but instead, her voice came out as a low groan as she toppled from her sitting position back onto the carnation comforter, her head hitting the pillow, the phone falling from her grasp onto the bed. Her head throbbed. The bedroom's décor inspired a childish antic, and she grabbed a pink, frilly pillow, and pulled it tightly around her face.

"Hello? Samantha? Hello?"

If Sam had been trying to avoid journalism by moving back to Birchwood, she hadn't been able to escape for long. It had literally run into her, at 12:15 p.m., on Sept. 3, in the form of a blue Honda.

Sam awoke to the beeping of her cell phone again; this time it was her 7:00 a.m. alarm. She pulled herself up out of bed, looking around the room. *Yep,* she thought, *not a dream. Still here.* She'd been rooming at her parents' place for the last six weeks, since she'd left Chicago.

She walked downstairs to find her mother preparing breakfast, the smell of warm pancakes drifting over from the griddle. It was a familiar scene. Bacon crackled and sputtered with grease in a pan on the stove. Late-summer sunlight illuminated her mother's kitchen—

small but inviting—in a golden glow. Roosters were everywhere, the kitchen's theme, according to Roselyn Hodges. A ceramic red bird perched on the stove, stenciled fowl ringed the ceiling molding like Sam's bedroom cats, and a large, homemade papier-mâché chicken sat proudly as the centerpiece at the wooden kitchen table, courtesy of one of Roselyn's habit of trying out new hobbies, that particular one dating back to 2012.

Sam sank into a seat. Her mother turned from where she poked at eggs in another pan. Roselyn's light brown hair was swept up at the back of her head, a pink long-sleeved shirt rolled to her elbows. She stood just two inches shorter than Sam, but her personality seemed to take up more room.

"Sam! How are you feeling? How is your head? We didn't want to wake you for dinner; I thought it best to let you sleep," she began, and Sam knew it was only the beginning. Sam reached behind her and half-closed a blue-checked curtain, her eyes squinting. "You've got a phone message from Frank Martin. He said you should come into the office today and that he has something to ask you. That's perfect—I can drop you off over there on my way to the supermarket. You know how your dad likes his Wheat Thins after the doctor said to stop eating potato chips, and I just can't keep enough of them in the pantry, it seems."

The deluge of chatter made Sam's head throb again. She pushed away the folded newspaper sitting in front of her, a *Bugle* copy that probably contained the brief about her incident from the day before. Birds squawked outside, and their chatter seemed especially high-pitched today.

"Don't you think eating three times as many Wheat Thins is about as good for you as snacking on potato chips?"

Roselyn ignored the question as she scooped a golden pancake, topped with glistening fresh strawberries, onto Sam's plate.

"You might say cake isn't the best thing to eat for breakfast, either," Roselyn said, a sly smile on her face. She knew Sam's soft spot for sweets.

Sam's stomach grumbled and she realized she hadn't eaten in almost 24 hours. She grabbed the maple syrup and drizzled it.

"Was Cathy Stilkington hurt?" she asked between forkfuls.

Roselyn frowned. "No, but they should have given her a higher fine, if you ask me. She could have hit anyone. Rolling through stop signs—you just can't ignore laws like that."

Sam crunched on a piece of bacon as her mother served her a steaming cup of coffee. The food felt good in her stomach, and the coffee began to ease her headache. It turned out that the signs of a concussion the doctor had told her about yesterday—slowed thinking, headache, lethargy—were also the signs of caffeine withdrawal.

While Sam ate, Roselyn untied her apron and loaded up the dishwasher with breakfast's pans and her mixers. She wiped down the white countertops with a rooster-printed dish towel which she flung over her shoulder before turning to Sam.

"So, you want a ride to the *Birchwood Bugle* office?"

"No, thanks." Sam swigged her coffee.

"Aren't you going to see what Frank wants to talk about? Maybe a job? The *Bugle* would be lucky to have your talents. And getting out of the house a bit more might be good for you. You can't spend all your time sulking."

Sam furrowed her brow. "I don't exactly think I'm the ideal hire after what happened. Anyway, I need the break."

"Well, a break can get boring, as your dad and I have found in retirement. You need something to keep your brain sharp, Sam. Why don't you try a different beat? Stay away from crime."

Roselyn talked so much that, often, she made at least a few good points. It was basic math; the odds were with her, Sam thought.

"Okay. I'll visit Frank to see what he wants to talk about," Sam said. "But I'll ride my bike."

Roselyn raised her eyebrows. "You watch out at those stop signs, miss."

Sam grabbed her empty plate and looked up at the wall clock. The roosters told her it was half past seven. She put the plate into the dishwasher and Roselyn put her hands on Sam's shoulders.

"Don't forget to wear your helmet."

"I won't," Sam said before turning to go back upstairs to get ready.

She decided she'd head out early; maybe she'd stop at the town café on the way for another coffee. Anything to get away from her mother's gentle nagging. As Sam climbed the stairs back to the second floor, she, for the first time, considered taking whatever job Frank might offer her, if Roselyn was right about that being his motive for the phone call. Maybe the small salary would allow her to get a place of her own in Birchwood, and a break from her parents: now that would be the ultimate rest.

Sam peeled out of her parents' driveway on the gray road bicycle she'd received as a college graduation present. She pedaled quickly, and considered briefly that she should have her guard up this time around. She had, after all, just been knocked unconscious by a two-ton battering ram less than 24 hours ago. But she'd ridden her bicycle around Chicago's busy streets, so Birchwood felt like a breeze, its streets tree-lined and the lawns vast. The size of the homes depended which side of the tracks you were on—the modest north side, or the opulent south. Birchwood was the last official suburb before the Chicago metropolitan area gave way to cornfields as far as the eye could see, and residents took advantage of the extra space, no matter the size of the homes they built. Sam sighed deeply as the wind rustled the green leaves. The space gave her room to breathe.

At the end of the block, Sam dutifully pulled to a stop at the red octagonal sign.

"Sam!" called a high-pitched voice. Sam turned over her shoulder to see her neighbor, Tammy Trembley, clad in a bright purple and yellow polka dot dress, huffing as she picked up her pace to reach Sam at the corner. The legs of her two tiny Yorkies, Macaroni and Cheese, whirred vigorously to keep up.

"Sam, I haven't been able to catch you at all this summer! You fly on that thing. Are you coming to my barbecue Wednesday night?"

Sam regretted obeying the stop sign. Sometimes, if you stopped in Birchwood, you might never get started again.

"I'm sure the whole family will be there, Mrs. Trembley," Sam said. "Got to go, sorry!" and she leaned into her pedals.

As Sam rode down Maple Lane, she vowed not to slow enough to let herself get caught up in small-town pleasantries. She pinpointed the possible conversation-starters: There was Hal Winters, father of Sam's best friend from high school, Greta. He ran the auto body shop in town. There was also Stacey Lynn, probably on her way to open the library, and Sam made a mental note to return all the detective novels she'd been voraciously reading while cooped up at her parents' place.

Cooped up. That's the right word for it, Sam thought. The ceramic red rooster on the top of the stove, his eyes bulging and his beak open mid-scream, flitted across her mind.

Sam kept an eye out for the familiar turn onto Grand Canine Way, the boulevard that led into Birchwood's downtown business district. The suburb was a mishmash of quintessential small-town Illinois naming conventions —towns and streets based on nature (River Road, Maple Lane, Reed Street)—and its newfound pet obsession

(Sugar Glider Street, Basset Boulevard, Animalia Avenue).

Though it was early, the sidewalks already had a few tourists and residents out and about giving their pets some exercise. Most visitors brought their pets with them to Birchwood, wanting to see the pet utopia they wished they had back home. They could take Rover to any restaurant, theater production, or gym class. They window-shopped at the designer dog clothing store and bought gourmet treats from any number of animal-friendly cafés. Their wide eyes and big smiles would have given them away as tourists if it weren't also for the prevalent fanny packs and visors.

Sam passed the cat café, Heaven Quinn's dog training academy, and Percy Harris' veterinary practice. Harris was the town's cat and dog specialist. There was also exotic animal veterinarian Owen Sanderson, alternative-medicine healer Valerie Viyasa, and livestock veterinarian Leo Ross.

Sam parked her bike at Hygge House and Hotel, the café and de facto town meeting place run by Greta Winters, and ran in to grab a coffee. Greta handed over Sam's 12-ounce dark roast, extra hot.

"Guess what?" Greta said, her blue eyes glowing with a mischievous look.

"Tell me." That was Sam's usual response, since it could be anything with Greta, and guessing was usually no use.

"One of my long-term tenants is moving out on floor two. You interested in the space?"

Sam immediately smiled. "Really, Greta? Those rooms get scooped up so fast."

"Not when my favorite VIP is back in town." Greta winked as a tourist pulled up beside Sam, his upturned face scanning the blackboard behind the counter. "What can I get for you?"

Sam mouthed goodbye and waved, turning to go. The coincidence of a room suddenly being available made Sam cross her fingers that she'd walk out of Frank Martin's office gainfully employed.

On her way out, Sam surveyed the regulars at Hygge House. A group of moms sat, bouncing babies on their knees and pushing strollers back and forth to soothe fussy infants. Usually at noon, a few of them in the constantly rotating gaggle promptly switched from cappuccinos and mocha frappés to wine. At a nearby booth, a few of the local dog shelter's employees sat before the start of the work day, their low whispers and furtive glances giving away their gossiping. A classmate of Sam and Greta's, Henry Jones, sat poring over something on his laptop, probably accounting spreadsheets, while Colleen Heath, his long-time girlfriend, chatted on the phone.

Sam exited Hygge House and bumped into Davis Yates, a young blogger in town.

"Oops, sorry," Yates muttered.

"It's okay," Sam said, but she was already speaking to the back of Yates' head as he brushed past her, continuing his fast and agitated walk. The young man was usually happy to share his latest concerns about his business, but today he seemed grumpy and preoccupied by something.

He had risen to prominence based on his fight to

make Birchwood's dog park the best in the nation. Barkington Beach was a proper dog park with water features, a sandy "beach," free tennis balls and a full-time staffed Pooper Scooper. (Poor Kenneth Buchanan, thought Sam, but it was an honest day's work for an honest day's wage.)

Yates was a closeted cat lover, the rumors said. You could find his old cat blog entries if you dug deep enough, but he'd learned quickly that dog lovers were more vocal and easier to organize ("herding cats," etc., etc.), and had switched to a team he could win with. Surprisingly, it had worked. Barkington Beach was no. 2 in the country, behind Paws Palace in Los Angeles.

Sam checked her takeaway coffee for spills around the lid and found none. It was only two blocks to the newspaper, so as usual she left her bike tied outside Hygge House and walked, passing by Sherry's Haircuts (Animal & Human), Rizzo's Italian Restaurant, and The Office, which was, ironically, a small, upscale bar. As she came up to the *Birchwood Bugle's* offices, she saw the small brick building with street-facing windows. She sipped her coffee, admiring the quaintness.

Renovation wasn't a part of the small-town newspaper budget, and the offices reminded Sam of the way all the stores in Birchwood had looked when she was a child. The building stood out among the newer, flashier storefronts. And the proximity of the *Birchwood Bugle's* offices to both other establishments meant a good flow of town gossip from ladies getting their hair done and men who had a few too many whiskeys.

Sam recognized Olaf, a giant St. Bernard, tied up outside of Kevin Frankfort's legal practice. He barked at

Sam, and she reached down to pat him. Being recognized —even by someone on four legs—was nice. She wondered what legal business his owner, Felicity Long, was up to inside. Or maybe she'd just run next door, to dog bakery Tails & Treats. Sam could still remember a decade ago when it was a fruit and vegetable store—for humans. She smiled at the memory.

Sam took a deep breath, her hand on her messenger bag strap. She hadn't been in a newsroom for six weeks, and it wasn't exactly a fond last day at the *Chicago Times* that she recalled. She took a last sip of her coffee and then walked up the steps, opened the door, and saw Wendy Billings' friendly face, framed by her long brown hair, held back by a headband, as always. Wendy looked no different than when she'd been the *Bugle's* receptionist when Sam had interned five years ago and was like a den mother to the cub reporters.

"Sam!" Wendy said, jumping up and embracing Sam's small frame and flouncy blonde locks in a hug. "I'm just so glad you're home. And visiting the *Bugle!*"

"It's really good to be back," Sam said, and she surprised herself by how much she meant it. There was something about the personableness of Birchwood that she hadn't realized she missed in the big city. No receptionist, let alone one she hadn't seen in years, had ever greeted her with a hug there.

Wendy took Sam's empty coffee cup from her and placed it in a small trash can before beaming at Sam. "All right. Let's get you to Frank."

CHAPTER ONE

The newsroom looked a lot like Sam remembered it. Unfortunately, that included the now ancient-looking computers, which had already been slow years ago. The floor was a drab gray, and local journalism awards were framed and hung on the walls, along with funny and favorite news clippings pinned on a large corkboard. Clusters of desks were laid out across the open office plan to form the different departments—crime, community, features, layout, and arts. *The photo cave must still be in the back corner,* Sam thought.

A few familiar faces looked up at Sam from their desks. She recognized Dale McLaughlin and Yolanda Oliver, the movie and food critics whose reviews Sam had been reading since she learned to put sentences together. (Roselyn had thought it scandalous whenever six-year-old Sam found reviews of R-rated films.) There was also Anne DeBraun, now the community news chief, who had worked in nearly every department at the paper.

At the crime desk cluster, Sam noticed Tom Albers'

reddish hair. He held a phone in the crook of his neck and shoulder, scribbling furiously on a notepad. Sam and Tom had interned together that summer years ago, but she hadn't known he was still at the paper. She smiled and waved, and Tom smiled back. She received a few smiles from some; others just watched her walk with Wendy through the newsroom to Frank's office against the back of the building. Sam suddenly hoped none of them recognized her. Or if they did, that it was from her writing. And not the viral videos.

A sudden wave of unease swept over Sam, and she began to feel a hint of lightheadedness. *It's just the residual effects of the concussion,* she convinced herself. But there was that nagging feeling—was a newsroom really the best place for her now? Her throat tightened.

"Oof," a voice said as someone bumped into Sam with a collection of camera and lens bags in the narrow walkway.

"Oh!" Sam said reflexively.

"James!" Wendy said. "How many times have I told you to watch where you're going?"

"I'm sorry, Wendy; I have to rush out to this scene right now," said a tall, brown-haired man with ocean-blue eyes.

"A crime scene?" Sam asked. Recognizing the frantic scramble of a photographer on his way out the door for breaking news, she began to get her bearings.

"More of an accident scene," James said, adjusting the many straps hanging from his neck. "Betty Palumbo's large bulldog got stuck in the children's slide at the community pool again."

Wendy rolled her eyes. "She's just doing it for the attention at this point. Really, is there not a way to leash him?"

"No man-made material can contain Bruno's excitement for water sports," James said.

"Except a plastic children's slide, it sounds like," Sam said, and James smiled. A beat of silence passed between them, and Wendy looked from one to the other.

"Sam," Sam said, extending her hand. "You better get to your breaking news."

"James," he said, shaking it. "See you later." He nodded at Wendy and was off.

Wendy shook her head, but whether at James, or Bruno, or Betty Palumbo, Sam couldn't tell.

"Here we are. I'm sure Frank will be excited to see you." Wendy gave Sam an encouraging shoulder squeeze, then turned and left.

Sam knocked. A moment later, she heard the familiar gravelly voice of her old editor.

"Come in."

Frank's office was as she remembered it, too, though Frank had more gray hair around the temples, and less hair altogether on the top of his head. His desk was its usual mess of papers, the shelves behind him full of maps, books, and histories of Birchwood. He stood behind his desk and extended his hand.

"Still riding that bike, huh?"

Sam gripped his hand and smiled. "I've been run over a few times; it's nothing."

Frank laughed. "Well, just watch out for trucks then."

He motioned for Sam to sit down, and finished writing a note on a piece of paper. Sam sat and put down her bag. She perched on the edge of the chair, then leaned back. She adjusted her arms, taking them on and off of the chair's arms. She waited.

"The news never slows!" Frank said finally, laying his pen down with a smack and looking up. "Nice to have you back in town, Samantha."

"It's been nice," Sam said, her voice stuck a bit in her throat. She cleared it. "It's ..." she searched for the right word. "... familiar."

"A newspaper can always benefit from someone who's familiar with the ins and outs of the town."

"Well, I don't get out much," Sam said, her voice soft. "I'm mostly familiar with my parents' house—with my mother's aviary." Sam could feel herself going on a bit of a tangent, but unable to stop. "Most of the conversations I've had in the last month have been with people who recognize me as Roselyn's daughter and ask about it."

Roselyn Hodges' budgerigar aviary was becoming legendary in Birchwood. It was her mother's newest pet project in her retirement, and Sam heard endlessly about the new ladder system, or bell-on-rope toys, or water filtration system being installed in the giant cage of parakeets. The birds' chirps and their bright feathers were also the perfect background soundtrack when Roselyn held her weekly morning tea sessions to gossip with the women-of-a-certain-age in town. Often, the gossip centered around the parakeets. Like a reality TV show, the trysts between the birds and their activities could be mined for endless scandal. Sam's mother would say she was having her friends over to watch "The Birdchelor" each week.

Frank nodded. "My wife tells me Princess is no longer preening with Reginald. She seems quite upset about it."

Sam's eyes widened. The aviary really did get to every corner of town, if Frank was hearing about it. How big had this pet thing in Birchwood gotten?

Frank leaned back in his chair and put his fingertips together. He had indulged Sam's tangent about birds, but directed the conversation back to the newspaper.

"How many years have you been a reporter now?"

Five years, Sam thought. How to condense the last five years into a response? It had been something she'd struggled with since being back in Birchwood, trying to find a clever soundbite. There was the internship after the *Bugle* at the *Minneapolis Daily,* then the *Los Angeles Post,* and finally, landing her dream job at the crime desk at the *Chicago Times.* Sam had worked relentlessly to cover the crime and mayhem that took place in Chicago, working the overnight shift on fires, store break-ins, and, unfortunately, murders. Then ...

"I was just fir—er, I left my position, at the *Chicago*— uh, the *Times,*" Sam sputtered. They'd technically placed her on leave, but had Sam rushed to cut her ties and run from the city.

Frank eyed Sam carefully. He leaned back, folding his hands together over his stomach.

"I think I'm taking a bit of a break from ... crime," Sam echoed her mother's words. If she couldn't find her own, there were always plenty of Roselyn's words to borrow.

"And how was working for Steve Harrison?"

Steve had been Sam's editor at the *Times*. And her boyfriend.

"I was his editor, back in the day. Sharp reporter, real sharp," Frank said. Frank always had compliments for anyone he worked with. Public relations professionals or public servants, however, he rarely had compliments for.

"He's great," Sam said with extra cheer. She blushed. "I feel like, um, my thank you for that reference letter you wrote is about five years overdue." She had forgotten that Frank had been a strong help in getting her the coveted position. Did he know the circumstances under which she had left?

"It can be hard to remember your hometown in the bright lights of the big city." Frank seemed wistful, like he was remembering something about his own past.

"Well, I'm here now, aren't I?" Sam said, a bit defiantly. She had expected people to see her as too good for Birchwood, coming back from a byline in a metropolitan newspaper. But she had a fierce love for the town, too. Despite its quirks. Frank was circling her with small talk, and she suddenly realized he was making her ask for the job. It made sense—if she couldn't ask for a job, how would she ask questions for a living?

Sam pulled her shoulders back and steadied her voice. Her burst of emotion at Frank's suggestion she'd forgotten Birchwood had helped. She tried to pretend she was Samantha Hodges, Crime Reporter for the *Chicago Times*, a job title that gave her a boost of confidence.

"You asked me in here today, I'm guessing, not to find out how Steve Harrison is doing." Frank waited. The silence trick. "Do you have a position open here?" Sam continued. "I'm interested," she paused, and then quickly added, "if you do."

"Finally, Hodges!" Frank banged his fist on his desk and Sam laughed with relief. "I've just gotten confirmation from our parent company that we have the extra budget for a position I've been pestering them about for six months. Pets Reporter!"

"Um, pardon?" Sam said.

"You just said yourself you were taking a break from crime. You wrote some wonderful light-hearted features for the *Bugle* as an intern."

"The story about the knitting circle? I can't seem to escape that one." A flash went through her mind of the two-page spread, framed and hanging back in the bedroom on Maple Lane, and the last day she'd spent with the knitting group. If only Frank knew how memorable that story had really been.

"I think you could do something great with the beat, if you applied yourself," Frank said.

Sam's brain felt like the wheels were turning a bit more slowly than usual. The only thing she could picture in her mind for "Pets Reporter" was burly Olaf, the St. Bernard, wearing a newsboy cap and a camera slung around his neck. Who would Sam Hodges, human Pets Reporter for the *Bugle*, be? Someone whose magnum opus had been a comprehensive look at catnip-toy knitters?

Sam looked down at her hands and thought it over.

Hiding in her parents' house for the last six weeks had been nice, but wrong for her. It wasn't anything close to applying herself. She was at her best out on the street, burning the shoe leather, talking to people.

She sighed, realizing there had been plenty of silence in Frank's office as she mulled over the offer. Looking up, she saw he was back to scribbling across a stack of papers. She'd give it a shot. She could always quit again—right?

"All right. I—"

"Glad to have you aboard," Frank cut in, not taking his eyes off the papers. "Henrietta Duveaux—I don't know if you know her—has had my phone ringing off the hook the last few weeks. Why don't you do a feature on her Retired Racer greyhound rescue?"

"An assignment already? On greyhounds?" It was becoming too real, too fast. She had a stack of detective novels to finish! "I just had a concussion yesterday."

"Mild, if my memory of the blotter copy serves me correctly. Here." Frank extended a piece of paper with a phone number scrawled on it. "Call her, so she stops calling me."

The paper hung in Frank's hand as Sam stared at it. What had she just done? Her work had been a matter of life and death in Chicago, and she wasn't ready for it to become a matter of kibbles and bits. Sam didn't know Henrietta Duveaux, so she'd need the phone number, and would have to look up her address. She took the paper, begrudgingly.

"Unless, of course, you're planning to return to Chicago," Frank said. Now he was looking at Sam and, she felt, right through her. Sam wasn't sure how to take his comment, and she cocked her head slightly, considering. Was it a threat about her leaving in embarrassment? Had Frank known she couldn't be choosy about assignments, so he had planned to trick her into this position all along? She felt herself blush, and an anger and steeliness coursed through her veins.

Sam took the paper, and Frank broke eye contact, going back to shuffling papers in the mess on his desk.

"So that's it, then?" Sam said.

"Thank you, Hodges." Frank glanced back up at her one more time.

Sam stood, holding the paper with Henrietta Duveaux's phone number carefully, like it was dynamite that might go off at any second. She looked at it. An assignment. Who'd have thought she'd be back in a newsroom, on a beat, so soon? But as Sam looked at the phone number, a familiar feeling rose in her. It was the possibility that a phone number scrawled hastily across a slip of paper offered. There was a story hiding in that number, and Sam wanted to draw it out and find it like hidden treasure. Frank needed a warm body in the Pets Reporter position, but if it was Sam who was going to fill it, she wasn't going to let herself—or the readers— down. She wasn't going to let her former self down either, who had worked hard for years building up this journalism career.

If Frank wanted a Pets Reporter, then he'd get one. Sam resolved to be the best Pets Reporter Birchwood had ever seen. The adrenaline of the decision still coursed through her as she turned toward the door.

"One more thing," Frank called as Sam reached the

office door. Sam turned back, hand on the knob. Frank smiled. "Welcome home."

~

Sam dialed Henrietta's number as she walked quickly through the newsroom, pulling out the reporter's spiral notebook and pen it was still a habit for her carry everywhere. She kept her head down, hoping no one would stop her. She'd rather they found out through the grapevine that she was the newest member of the staff. *And the Pets Reporter to boot,* Sam thought, *running around sniffing out a greyhound story.*

The call was picked up just as Sam waved goodbye to Wendy and stepped out onto the sidewalk.

"Hello?" Henrietta's voice was high and sweet, and had a slight European accent, though Sam couldn't identify the country.

"Hello, Miss Duveaux? My name is Sam Hodges. I'm calling from the *Bugle.* I'm the—" Sam rolled her eyes. "I'm the Pets Reporter."

"Finally, some sense has been knocked into someone over there! I can't tell you how glad I am that you called. Now let me see. Where was it?" Sam heard rustling papers in the background and once again passed Olaf outside the legal practice, as she made her way back to her bicycle. He wagged his tail.

"I can come over right now to discuss—" Sam began.

"I have a document I think a reporter would like to see. Very controversial, so I'd like you to handle it with the utmost care, of course, but we can discuss it more in person," Henrietta said.

"Great. I'll be right ove—"

"Oh! Someone's at the door. I'm so sorry, Sam, was it?" Henrietta laughed. "Come over tonight, after the dogs are all fed so they won't be barking up a storm while we're trying to talk. Okay! Okay! I'm coming! 6:30 should be good. See you then."

The line went dead. Sam shook her head. So the greyhound story might be harder to sniff out than she'd expected. She'd need to double-down on this whole Pets Reporter thing.

CHAPTER TWO

Sam's thighs burned as she turned her bicycle up a gear. Henrietta's home and the connected Retired Racer Rescue were gently tucked away in a non-flashy residential section of town, on the more modest north side where Sam's parents lived. But the ride was a good few miles, and not on friendly terrain. Wichitaw Way, the street Henrietta lived on, was the only unpaved street in Birchwood. If Sam followed it for another half hour, she'd arrive at the Birchwood Zoo, where her older sister worked. Frances might know a bit about the pet world in Birchwood, and Sam made a mental note to call her after the interview with Henrietta.

Sam had spent the day at Greta's Hygge House café, researching the Retired Racer Rescue online. There was no website—though that wasn't unheard of for the older businesses in town. There was a 2008 story from the *Chicago Times* that came up, and Sam had winced looking at the familiar masthead. The story said that, in the midst of a lot of tornado destruction across many rural towns in Illinois, Henrietta had taken in nine grey-hounds, eventually reuniting five with their owners and finding permanent homes for three more when their owners didn't step forward. That had been years ago, so Sam figured the last storm dog wasn't still living at the rescue. If he was, it would be the makings of a great story, so Sam hoped against the odds that he might still be.

Now that the sun was setting, there was a chill in the air, autumn warning Sam that it was soon to arrive. She pumped her legs and took a turn onto Wichitaw Way sharply. A greyhound shot past her front wheel. Sam lost control of her handlebars, trying to keep the bicycle steady, but the front wheel turned in the dirt.

"Aghhh!" Sam yelled as she twisted to her side, trying her best not to land on her head. She felt the pavement first, hitting her hip and then her shoulder. The metal of her road bike swiftly followed, banging her on the shins. The fall felt like it took a full minute to Sam, but it must have only been a second. Everything went black.

Sam blinked and opened her eyes, looking at the sky above. Had she just been hit by Cathy Stilkington, and all this Pets Reporter nonsense had been a dream? A dog barked nearby.

A long, slim snout came into Sam's view. Round, amber eyes looked at her. Sam sat up, scraped, and sure to be sore later, but on the whole, uninjured. A beautiful brindle-colored greyhound stood next to her, wagging its whip-like tail. The dog sniffed the air in front of it, leaning forward a bit. The greyhound seemed curious as to who Sam was, this person now sitting at dog-level.

"Pumpernickel." Sam reached out and read the dog's

name tag. There was no address, but Sam could guess where she'd come from. "I think we're headed in the same direction, Pumpernickel."

Sam walked the last three blocks with her bicycle while the dog dutifully followed behind her. Sam came to a single-story home and double-checked the address she'd found on file for Henrietta. 518 Wichitaw Way. This was it. Henrietta's home was small, but the land it sat on was large. Extensive barking came from behind the house. So much for quiet after the dogs were fed.

There was no doorbell; Sam knocked on a large red door. She noticed at the same time that she knocked that the door was slightly ajar. With her rap, it swung open further. Pumpernickel raced through.

"Hey!" Sam said. "Miss Duveaux," she called through the slit. "Miss Duveaux! It's Sam Hodges. From the newspaper. I found one of your dogs."

Had Henrietta forgotten their appointment? No one seemed to be home. All the lights were off.

Well, now that the rogue dog had burst through the doors, Sam would need to find her. She realized there hadn't been anything on the collar to identify the rescue as her home, and perhaps she was someone else's escaped greyhound now wandering around inside Henrietta's place.

"Henrietta!" Sam called again before dialing Henrietta's number. Inside the house somewhere, she heard a phone ringing and ringing.

Sam pushed the door open a bit wider when there was no response.

"Pumpernickel?"

Sam walked inside and clicked on the flashlight on her phone, dusk settling around the house and turning everything a dusty, flat hue. Sam swept the light over the room. The décor looked like it hadn't been updated in decades, if the shag carpet was any indication. It was even older than Roselyn's. Sam looked for a light switch and clicked it on.

From the entryway light, she could see a living room, street-facing, to her right. Up ahead looked like a kitchen. A door to her left, closed, she figured by process of elimination, was Henrietta's bedroom.

"Hello?" Sam called out again.

In the living room, Sam could see hundreds of dogs: every surface was covered in pictures of greyhounds. She walked into the room and bent down to look at the collection on an end table. The frames had names painted across the bottom: Scotch, Timmy, Tabitha. Sam wondered just how many dogs had come through this rescue. It could amount to hundreds, if all the pictures were of different dogs. The sheer number could be an impressive angle for her story.

Sam jumped when something wet pressed into her hand. Pumpernickel whined beside her.

"I'm not snooping," Sam said. "It's research for a story. And now that I've found you, we can both get out of here."

Sam reached for Pumpernickel's collar but the dog stepped away, lifting her feet in a rhythm as though in a nervous dance. She whined again, then turned and jogged a few steps before stopping to look at Sam. *Are you following?* her eyes seemed to say.

Sam sighed. In her experience, animals were rarely cooperative. Not logical, like humans. Well, not all humans were logical. Why was this old lady leaving her home unlocked? And the door open?

"Henrietta!" Sam called again. She heard barking from the dogs out back once more, and wondered if they had been fed. Where *was* Henrietta? Sam didn't like feeling like she was breaking in, but something kept propelling her forward. Something felt off.

Sam walked through Henrietta's kitchen, in the direction which Pumpernickel had disappeared again, and was once again submerged in near-darkness. A faint light from the entryway fell into the tiny, outdated eatery with mint-green plastic countertops, and Sam saw Pumpernickel's whip tail slip through the back door, which was also slightly ajar.

Sam heard a slam from the front of the home. She turned swiftly around to look at the entryway, which was a straight shot back through the kitchen. The front door had closed; it was probably the wind. Sam jumped as another sound came from behind her, this time, a sharp bark. She whirled around and her flashlight shone on the back door, revealing a small snout poking through the gap.

"Okay, *okay!*" Sam said, as though she was a teenager being asked to pick up her room for the fortieth time.

Sam walked out into the backyard and could hear the barking of many dogs and their shuffling bodies. She swung her flashlight around, but couldn't illuminate very far in front of her with the paltry phone light. There was no pathway, just grass beneath her Converse, and the giant silhouettes of trees rustling in a breeze that was picking up.

Sam heard Pumpernickel's bark; it sounded closer than the other dogs'. Or did she somehow already recognize Pumpernickel's voice out of the cacophony?

Sam made her way forward, and then a bright light flooded the entire backyard. Sam could see a dozen or so dogs up a small hill, each in a kennel, some pawing at their gates and barking. Half of them cowered in the shadows. In front of them, though, closer to Sam and the house, was a wagon, tipped on its side, dog food bowls spilled onto the earth.

Pumpernickel stood behind the wagon, barking.

As Sam moved closer, she could see an outstretched arm.

Sam's heart leapt and she quickened her steps.

Arriving at the wagon and food mess, she saw the woman she recognized from the photos online, but a bit older. Henrietta was wearing a long skirt and a flowy teal shirt. A golden-patterned shawl that had once been around her shoulders now lay tucked just under her arm, most of it blowing in the breeze. A flashlight lay in one still hand. A dark liquid was spreading out from near her head.

A feeling began creeping up the back of Sam's neck, and it took her a moment to recognize it, a sensation she had been used to as a reporter: the grimness of a crime scene before her. Sam couldn't tell if her hunch was right, but something about the scene told her, from her years on the crime beat, that this wasn't just a little old lady who had fallen. Sam glanced around the backyard. Besides the dogs, there was no one.

Sam knelt down. "Henrietta?" She lifted the old lady's wrist to check for a pulse, and Henrietta's skin was cold to the touch. She looked up at Henrietta's face, pale gray and slack. Almost peaceful. But not quite. There was the slightest furrowing of Henrietta's brow, as though she had died disappointed, her mouth turned down.

Pumpernickel crept forward, her chin resting over Sam's shoulder. Sam felt nothing; there was no pulse. Sam pulled her hand back quickly. She swallowed as she stood up and pulled her phone out of her pocket. Pumpernickel whined.

Sam waited, and then a woman picked up on the other end of the line.

"911, what's your emergency?" the operator asked.

"I'm at 518 Wichitaw Way," Sam said. "And I think Henrietta Duveaux is dead."

CHAPTER THREE

The police arrived quickly after Sam's call. The scene felt familiar: the blue and red flashing lights of the squad cars, the ambulance and fire truck arriving as they always did in any emergency, the crisp navy-blue uniforms of the officers, the crackle of their radios. Sam was used to arriving at a crime scene with this other life bubbling around her—the police, ambulances, onlookers. Compared to it, the stillness of the backyard, Henrietta's gravesite, was eerie. Sam had never been the one to *find* the bodies as a crime reporter. She had arrived later, like all the other mortality professionals, maintaining a professional distance.

After the police arrived, they asked Sam to wait in the living room as they tended to the scene. Sam sat on the cream, paisley-printed couch and looked at the hundreds of dogs scattered all over the walls. She marveled at the sheer rainbow of colors greyhounds could be. Their fur shone white, gray, black, and even muted oranges, reds, and blues. Pumpernickel, her own fur brindle-striped in gray, white, and black, curled up on the couch next to her.

As Sam looked around the room, something glistened underneath an end table, shining out from in between the strands of another shag carpet like the one Sam had first noticed in the entryway. Sam moved her head from side to side, trying to make it out, but she couldn't. She walked over, bent down, and reached for the shiny object.

Sam saw that it was a green pacifier, still wet with a few drops of spittle. *What's this doing here?* Sam thought. It seemed out of place in a home that felt more like a mausoleum than a daycare. Sam remembered the person who had interrupted her phone call with Henrietta. So she'd had an unexpected visitor earlier that day.

She turned the pacifier this way and that, inspecting it like an alien object. To a 26-year-old without even a boyfriend, it might as well have been. Sam stood, still looking at the pacifier intently, as though it might shout at any moment, "I did it!"

A man cleared his throat loudly. Sam jumped and reflexively stuffed the pacifier in her pocket as though she had been caught stealing cookies.

Sam turned and a tall man with brown eyes and short, dark hair, wearing a police uniform, entered the room. He motioned toward the couch, next to Pumpernickel, and Sam returned to her seat.

"Detective Jasper," the man in uniform said as he sat down next to Sam. "How are you doing, um ... Samantha? You knew Miss Duveaux?"

"We spoke on the phone but I'd never met her."

The detective asked about Sam finding the body and

she relayed the events of the evening. She went over their planned meeting (neglecting to mention her Pets Reporter role), the open doors, and the loose dog. Pumpernickel pawed at Sam's leg when she mentioned her name.

"Our police force doesn't have an on-staff psychologist, but I took some courses in college, so if you feel like you need to talk to someone, you can talk to me." Jasper did his best to look sympathetic, but Sam felt that he was contorting his face all wrong for the emotion.

She looked at him but said nothing, reflecting. *Dan.* She suddenly recognized him. Dan Jasper. He had been four grades older than Sam. Dan's little brother, Steven, had been in her class. She felt more confident being able to place him. She had come to recognize most of the police officers she saw at crime scenes in Chicago, but she hadn't gone to school with any of their younger brothers. The recognition grounded her back in Birchwood, overpowering the flashing police lights that made her feel like she was back in Chicago.

"Just in case you need to, uh, process your experience," Jasper added. It sounded like something from a crisis response brochure.

Sam shuddered to think of all the professional services that had been recommended to her after her breakdown in Chicago. She maintained a steady voice. "That's so kind and professional of you, officer—"

"Detective."

"Detective," Sam repeated. "But I think I'm really okay. It would make me feel better to know, though, how will the police be investigating this death?"

Jasper straightened up, seemingly pleased not to have to provide spontaneous therapy. "We can't rule out any possibilities, but at that woman's age, there are a number of things that could go wrong, naturally."

Natural causes? Sam recognized this as a crime scene; shouldn't the seasoned detective? She'd had time in the five minutes before the ambulance tires squealed up to 518 Wichitaw Way to look over the scene, snapping immediately into crime reporter mode like she had never left it. By the odd way Henrietta's body had been lying, Sam felt almost certain she had been killed. A person didn't fall naturally like that from a heart attack, even if she bumped her head on the way down. And why was the wagon and all the dog food spilled? It looked like there had been a struggle.

Sam began piecing together the sequence of events in her mind. Henrietta had been in the middle of feeding the dogs when she was killed. Pumpernickel's kennel was open because Henrietta had been preparing to place her food bowl in her cage. It had never made it, if the spilled food bowl next to Henrietta's hand was any indication. There was no murder weapon that Sam could see, but she guessed Henrietta had been hit over the head with something.

The automatic floodlights had come on when Sam had entered the backyard, so why had Henrietta needed a flashlight? Had someone disabled them? And why had all her home's doors been open? Jasper's voice derailed Sam's train of thought.

"We've called someone to come take care of the dogs," he said.

Sam realized her hand was resting on Pumpernickel's head, which was resting on Sam's leg.

"I know how you people in town get all worked up about animals. They will be looked after, don't you worry." Jasper said, in an attempt at a soothing voice, but one that came out condescending instead. The way he said "you people," and "worked up" made Sam feel suddenly very hot around her neck and chest. One could be apathetic about animals in Birchwood, but one couldn't go around insulting everyone in Birchwood who wasn't.

"Especially this one." Detective Jasper suddenly stood, his eyes growing wide, pointing at Pumpernickel. "*This* dog—this is who has been getting blood all over my investigation scene all night!"

Sam noticed for the first time that Pumpernickel's back left leg had a small cut on it, dripping a bit of blood on the couch.

"Someone get this dog out of here!" Jasper yelled towards the kitchen, where two other officers were sipping coffee. "Johnson? Is that woman here yet? Hello!"

Sam took the opportunity to get out her notebook and scrawl:

Floodlights? Flashlight

Open doors

Pumpernickel scratch

No murder weapon

Police investigating as accident? (really???)

With notebook in hand, in the presence of police, Sam said out of habit, "And the time of death, Detective?"

Jasper turned back to her, his eyes narrowing at the site of her pen over her notebook and her expectant face.

"What are you, a reporter?" he said.

Sam recognized the note of disdain in Jasper's voice. Sam had come across quite a few police officers in Chicago who were great to work with, but the large majority saw journalists as pesky vultures buzzing around death, their questions an annoyance more than a public good.

Sam stood and extended her hand with poise, a defiant smile creeping over her face. "Samantha Hodges. Pets Reporter for the *Birchwood Bugle*, sir."

Sam powerwalked out of Henrietta's house, still hearing Jasper's angry shouts behind her. He certainly loved to yell. For being a detective, he didn't seem to have the easiest way with people.

As Sam walked down the path from Henrietta's front door, a woman in an orange fleece vest and old jeans appeared outside the front gate and unlatched it with practiced precision. Sam hadn't noticed the gate when she and Pumpernickel had first approached Henrietta's house; the door must have been swung wide open. The woman headed in Sam's direction, dirty work boots striding purposefully.

"Pumpernickel!" the woman said, and Sam looked behind her to see Pumpernickel following closely. Pumpernickel leapt forward. Kneeling to examine the dog, the woman looked up at Sam. "Is she okay?"

"She has a small scratch, but other than that, she seems to be acting normally," Sam offered.

"I got a call from police to come for an emergency," the woman said, standing once more. Pumpernickel pawed at her pant leg and the woman reached her arm down to scratch the dog's head. She looked stricken. "Do you know what happened? Are more dogs hurt?"

Her concerned frown deepened so Sam could see the wrinkles around her mouth.

"Dana Tripp?" Sam guessed. She had written Dana's phone number down in her hasty look around the house before the police arrived, noting her as one of two "Emergency Contacts" on Henrietta's fridge, along with Percy Harris.

Dana nodded. "I'm her only employee." Dana looked around at the flashing lights of the squad cars, and back at Sam. "Are you police?"

"Sam Hodges, Pets Reporter for the *Bugle*," The introduction was starting to become a reflex. "Interviewing Henrietta was my first assignment. I hate to be the one to tell you this, Dana, but Henrietta has had an accident and—"

"Oh my gosh, she insists on letting the greyhounds run around her all the time," Dana said, waving her hands in the air. "She wants to give them 'people time,' which is great for their recovery from racing, but at her age, and their speed, she trips over them all the time! She broke her arm last year; sprained her ankle the year before. What is it this time?"

"Dana, I'm so sorry." Sam swallowed. In Chicago, people often knew what flashing lights arriving on their doorstep meant. In Birchwood, maybe not. "Henrietta is dead."

Dana's face went blank. She seemed to be looking at something behind Sam. Sam turned and looked behind her. The house was lit up, but betrayed no other indication of what had happened there.

Sam turned back to Dana, whose face had now started to crumple.

Sam began what she hoped would be a comforting spiel. "I know it must be difficult to—"

Dana shook her head and held up her hand. "I feel so bad ..." Dana trailed off. She knelt down again and took Pumpernickel's face in her hands. Pumpernickel licked her tears. "What's going to happen to the dogs?"

CHAPTER FOUR

S am tried to sneak in a sip of her latte, which was quickly cooling on the café table.

"And you're here to talk to me about …" she asked the man sitting across from her as she brought the bright blue mug to her lips. The latte art—a cartoonish cat face, one of Greta's signatures—was pristine, untouched.

"It's like there was an explosion of squirrels on Westward Avenue," he said a bit gruffly. In her mind, Sam pictured a sonic boom of squirrels, bushy tails and tiny paws flying through the air, landing on maple tree branches and cottage roofs all down the lane. She sipped, considering the scenario. The man apparently took her silence as encouragement.

"The neighbors say my boy Baxter barks at the squirrels too much, but I say, if we had more dogs like Baxter on the street, we wouldn't *have* the squirrel problem in the first place! Overpopulation of one mammal is bad for the Westward Avenue ecosystem. And I know for a fact that Mrs. Byrd down the street is feeding those squirrels

Ritz crackers. I've seen her do it! Ritz! You know what else is bad for the ecosystem, besides overpopulation?"

"Ritz?" Sam asked, swallowing her lukewarm coffee.

"Ritz!" he said. "That's too many carbs for those little guys." The man leaned back and shook his head as though a ton of carbo-loaded tree rodents was the greatest tragedy he'd ever seen. Sam might have been surprised that this large, middle-aged man wearing a flannel shirt was concerned about a small animal. But of course, this was Birchwood.

"I'm starting to think the little rascals are organizing, too," the man said. He pointed to Sam's notepad and pen. "Are you taking notes, by the way?"

Sam nodded, her mouth full. She had tried to sneak in another bite of her cooling breakfast. In front of her were fresh eggs Benedict in Greta's signature spicy hollandaise. The perfectly poached eggs sat atop fresh pink salmon slices, and the dish was extra delicious with the added bonus of a fluffy, freshly-baked croissant swapped in for the English muffins. On the side, Sam had one of Greta's freshly-baked caramel rolls, a cinnamon-coated breadstick with caramel drizzle on top. Sam looked longingly at her caramel roll, which was missing a bite, as Sam was always one to eat sweet before savory. But she instead grabbed her notebook and scrawled some of the highlights of the pressing squirrel issue.

"And your name?" she asked.

"John Lowe," the man said as he stood and offered his phone number. "And Samantha, thanks, by the way. I don't know why the newspaper hadn't hired someone with your background before to cover the four-legged residents of this town. You're doing us all a great service."

Sam stood and shook his outstretched hand. She smiled, having forgotten how it felt to get appreciation from readers.

As John Lowe walked away, Sam saw Lawrence Everton, the town aquarium expert, walk into the coffee shop carrying a folded copy of the *Birchwood Bugle* under his arm. Sam could see the small square on the corner of the front page that detailed the death of Henrietta Duveaux. Her smile faded. She sat back down at the table, her favorite, near the front window, great for people-watching.

The paper had also printed an article this morning, buried on page 11, introducing Sam as the Pets Reporter, and that had gotten much more attention than the front-page death of a reclusive old woman on the edge of town. Residents had been abuzz ever since with story ideas for Sam. Not much had been said about Henrietta.

Sam had hoped for a quiet, early (and caramel-coated) breakfast at Hygge House to go over her notes from the night before. It had been a late night after taking Pumpernickel to Percy Harris for her scratch, at Dana's request.

"And if you could maybe foster her for a few days while I sort out all of this," Dana had said, assuming that Sam, of course, had the capability to take in a dog, as she probably had several pets of her own.

So now Sam was not only a Pets Reporter, but had a temporary pet of her own. Roselyn had fawned so much over the new animal that Sam had been able to evade specific questions about how Pumpernickel had come into her care.

Sam slipped Pumpernickel a bite of egg as the dog sat attentively next to her. Like most establishments in Birchwood, Hygge House & Hotel was pet-friendly.

That Henrietta's murder didn't draw attention made Sam wonder if she was imagining things. Was the disgraced crime reporter being just a little too quick to assume grisly Chicago crime was also present in this sleepy, quaint town?

"You don't look at all like your picture, darling," a woman's voice said, and Sam looked up. If she covered every story idea that had interrupted her breakfast that morning, she'd have no time remaining to ponder Birchwood's crime rate.

"That picture is from years ago," Sam said to the middle-aged woman with her auburn hair pulled back into a tight bun. The woman placed the folded newspaper down in front of Sam, open to page 11. On the bottom was Sam's picture, next to the headline, "*Chicago Times reporter, Birchwood native, to spearhead Pets coverage.*" The picture the paper had used of her was from when she'd interned for the *Bugle* at age 21, sporting straight, long, dark red hair. Now that she'd let her naturally blonde hair recover for five years from all the ill-advised college dye jobs, its springy curl had returned.

"It frames your face very nicely now," the woman said. Sam could tell that she was dropping the kind of compliment people did before they asked a favor.

"Mrs. Peters, how lovely to see you." Greta appeared

at Sam's table. "I just delivered your French Toast to your table; you better dig in before it gets cold."

"Oh, thank you, Greta. I was just about to tell Sam about Dr. Pibbles' flu fundraiser. It would be nice to raise some money. Mostly awareness of feline flu. But also his vet bills. They are so—"

"Thanks, Mrs. Peters, I'll look into it," Sam said, jotting down notes. Mrs. Peters returned to her table and Sam turned to Greta.

"Is Dr. Pibbles a new vet?"

"That's her cat," Greta said. "I wouldn't go to him for medical advice."

"You know, people in Chicago didn't like talking to reporters a lot of the time. Here, I can't seem to stop people from talking to me." Sam took a bite of the caramel roll.

"Sam, I've seen more wallet photos of dachshunds than children in this town." Greta pointed to Sam's cold eggs Benedict, the hollandaise hardening. "I've got a few minutes before the morning rush; I can remake that food," Greta offered.

Sam waved her hand. "It's delicious hot or cold, Greta."

Greta wiped her hands on her apron and sat down at Sam's table.

"How's the beat?" she asked.

"Deadly," Sam said.

Greta raised her eyebrows at Sam as she picked up a fork in the practiced "May I have some?" that didn't need explaining between two old friends.

Sam nodded as Greta cut off a piece of egg, salmon, and croissant.

"You interviewing pest control?" Greta asked.

"No, I went out to interview Henrietta Duveaux last night," Sam began.

"The greyhound lady?"

"You knew her?"

"*Knew* her?" Greta frowned. "Wait. Is she the one who's dead?"

"I found the body," Sam said, stone-faced. She leaned forward. "And I think someone might have killed her."

"No!" Greta said loudly in disbelief. Her eyes were wide. "I thought you moved back here to get away from all that murder stuff."

"Sort of," Sam said noncommittally.

Greta was the type of friend who could tell when you were thinking about your ex-boyfriend. "And to get away from Steve Harrison." There was a glint in her eye.

Sam glanced around the café; gossip spread like wildfire in Birchwood.

"Don't worry," Greta said. "Mason Reed doesn't care."

The middle-aged man in a large navy windbreaker, eating at the table nearest them, looked up and smiled. "Sure don't," he said.

"Hey, Mason, did you know Henrietta Duveaux was found dead last night?" Greta said.

"Greta—"

"Sam found her body!" She pointed across the table at Sam.

Several more café patrons turned to look.

"Shame," Mason said, though it looked to Sam like he really didn't think it was a shame at all. He went back to reading his newspaper.

"Thanks, Greta, that will be sure to get the whole town talking." Sam rolled her eyes and grabbed her fork back.

"Well, there's no better way to solve a murder," Greta replied.

"Are you still watching those crime shows?" In high school, Greta had been obsessed with *Law & Order*, *NCIS*, *CSI*, and a host of other shows Sam didn't even know the names—or acronyms—of.

"I've seen all the episodes, pretty much," Greta said. "But the reruns are always good. When you know who the killer is, looking back on the story, it's so obvious." A family with three daughters and four dachshunds entered the café, and both Sam and Greta turned to look at the hubbub. "Okay, the morning rush has officially begun! See you later, sweet peeps. You too, sweet feet," she said, patting Pumpernickel. "I'll bring you a treat in a little bit."

Greta was always coming up with nicknames like that for the café patrons. If the food wasn't the driving force at Hygge House, it might be Greta herself. She always put on a show, dancing around the café and delighting customers. Sam knew Greta figured Sam had been joking about Henrietta's murder. Greta herself often did the same. Anytime anyone in town showed up with a sprained wrist or twisted ankle, Greta created elaborate stories about who had tried to kill them.

When their woodshop teacher in middle school, Mr.

Garber, had had a sling for two months, Greta had been convinced his wife wanted him out of the picture. "Look," she'd whispered one day, pointing to the family photo of Mr. Garber with his wife and their two sons. "I don't trust her eyes."

"I don't trust her forehead," Sam had said, and the two had laughed for years about their private joke.

Sam opened her notebook with the notes about Henrietta's death. She saw Detective Jasper's name and felt a small surge of anger. *Now that's a forehead I really don't trust,* she thought. She flipped back through a few pages to her notes from when she'd first spoken on the phone with Henrietta to set up their interview. She recalled Henrietta's visitor, and Sam's hand moved quickly to her jacket pocket, where she had stored the green pacifier from the night before.

She pulled it out and looked at it. She should have left it for Detective Jasper to find, was her first thought, but her second was that it was too late now, and she might as well get some information from it. His untrustworthy forehead would have to wait. Sam flagged down Greta once more.

"Greta, one of the mothers must have dropped this. Would you mind returning it to them?"

"Oh, gross," Greta said. "Probably covered in dog hair." Greta grabbed the pacifier, stuffed it in her apron pocket, and delivered the Croque Monsieur and Croque Madame she was carrying to a table of two. Sam watched her approach the mothers' group and hold out the pacifier. There were four of them: a straight-haired blonde, a wispy dark-haired woman, a woman with a messy brown bun, and one woman wearing a jogging outfit and sipping a coffee to-go.

The mothers looked around at each other and the dark-haired woman reached for the pacifier. But so did the straight-blonde-haired one. They looked at each other and seemed to quibble a bit, and then the blonde-haired woman shrugged and the dark-haired woman grabbed it after all.

Sam scribbled down a quick description of the mothers, as she didn't recognize any of them from growing up in Birchwood. She made a note to catch Greta before she left and find out their names.

Someone came into Sam's peripheral vision, standing at her table. She set down her pen, sighed, and raised her head. "You have a story for—"

But the short, pudgy man with sandy hair at her table wasn't looking at her. He was looking out the café window and pointing at something. Sam turned her head and saw nothing but Grand Canine Way, the main business strip in downtown Birchwood, beginning to wake.

Then a few flashes of color dashed past. Gray, white, a muted red.

Chairs scratched against the hardwood of Hygge House as people stood to watch. Some gasped.

"Dogs!" someone shouted.

"Greyhounds," Sam added gravely.

The *Bugle's* newspaper delivery man, George McCarter, was the next to zoom past the front of the shop, albeit more slowly than the dogs. He pumped his arms, fingers out flat, like an Olympic sprinter.

"*Mailman chases dog.* That's your headline right

there," said Mason Reed, who was still sipping a hot cup of something.

Sam leapt to her feet and started gathering all her things. She stuffed the last bite of caramel roll in her mouth, slung her messenger bag over her shoulder, and was grabbing her phone and her bicycle lock key as a fourth dog, cream-colored, trotted out front, its long tongue lolling from its mouth. Four people raced from the restaurant to help: Sam, Henry Jones, Colleen, and the father of the dachshund family, the one with three daughters and four dogs that had entered the café earlier, to much hubbub.

Sam stopped and stood by the bicycle rack out front and dialed Dana Tripp. Pumpernickel performed her feet-up dance again, and Sam feared the worst. The last time she'd seen her do that, she had found Henrietta's body minutes later. As the phone rang, Sam watched Dachshund Dad and Henry Jones try to corner the cream-colored greyhound at the entrance to Danielle's Every Day Dog Wear. But the greyhound dove between Henry's legs and raced back in the direction it had come from.

Across the street, near the railroad tracks that led into Chicago, George McCarter hugged a red greyhound weighing no more than 25 pounds to his chest. The satisfied smile on George's face faded as the dog wriggled free from his grip then ran around him in circles.

The phone rang and rang, but there was no answer. Sam hung up and called the photo desk at the *Bugle* instead.

"Hi, James? It's Sam." Sam suddenly became aware

of her heart beating rapidly in her chest. Probably because she hadn't seen the pandemonium of breaking news in six weeks. "I think you'll want to get photos of this downtown. Or send a reporter. Um, it's dogs. Well, dogs running everywhere. People chasing them. Oh, geez, um, I'm not selling it well. But I think it will be good. I have to run, though. See you in the office later."

Sam hung up and took a deep breath. She usually wasn't so unclear when breaking news was happening. Maybe because it was pets. She had a long way to go if she was going to be the best Pets Reporter Birchwood had ever seen. Sam hopped on her bicycle and began to pedal towards the Retired Racer Rescue.

CHAPTER FIVE

Pumpernickel had no trouble keeping up pace with Sam's cycling as the two followed the path to the Retired Racer Rescue, passing by the fateful spot where the young woman and dog had met—and collided—the night before.

Sam walked up to Henrietta's backyard, where the kennels were, and noticed there was a clear view of Henrietta's yard from the house next door, albeit at a bit of a distance. Sam also saw five dogs jumping around the yard as Dana tried to lead each one to its kennel, rushing in big rain boots from one end of the dog run to the other.

Dana waved her arms and declared, "I didn't think it would be this hard all by myself!"

Sam cleared her throat. "Got a mutiny on your hands?"

Dana spun around. "Have you found another one? Oh, Pumpernickel. It's you." Dana had a habit of addressing the dog more than Sam.

"A few people are trying to catch the dogs down near

Hygge House," Sam called. "I'm sure they'll get back here in one piece. Here, I'll ask my photographer to send me updates."

Sam opened a new message to James' number.

Please send updates about dogs. At Rescue now with worried employee. Thanks :)

Then Sam bit her lip. She deleted the smile. She deleted everything.

Hi James, can you send me updates when the dogs are safe? Would be a big help. Thank you!

Sam started to delete it again, but then stopped herself and pressed send. A bright white greyhound, the largest Sam had seen yet, trotted over and poked its nose through the wire fence to greet Pumpernickel. At the same time, Sam noticed a wheelbarrow turned on its side within the fence of the rescue—a fence with a large hole in it, she realized.

"Is this how they got out?" Sam pointed to the hole.

Dana stopped chasing a dog as it zoomed out of her grasp. She walked over and sighed deeply.

"Yes," Dana said. "They've never gotten out before. Things are getting crazy around here, and the dogs seem hyped up as well. Out of sorts. I'm a bit overwhelmed."

Sam eyed the hole in the fence. Maybe Dana was too frazzled to notice, but it definitely hadn't been dug up by the dogs. That was a man-made hole. Probably wire cutters. If it had been cut the night of Henrietta's murder, the dogs would have escaped then. So who had come to the rescue just to cut a hole in the fence? Sam couldn't imagine the two crimes weren't connected, or more likely, committed by the same person.

"Can I help?" Sam asked.

A few tears fell from Dana's eyes. It was the second time Sam had seen Dana cry in 24 hours, but it was understandable after Henrietta's death, though Dana didn't seem too preoccupied with that.

"Thank you, Sam. I'm just so worried about them," Dana said. She unlocked the gate and led Sam and Pumpernickel through while holding back the other dogs.

"And it's hard all by yourself?" Sam prompted.

Dana nodded solemnly as she surveyed the dogs before her.

Sam wanted to ask Dana about where she had been the night of the murder, but she knew she'd have to walk a careful road to get to that point. Then Sam realized she was the Pets Reporter. She had the best tool in the world to start asking endless questions. Sam opened her messenger bag and pulled out her small black voice recorder.

"Dana, I'm writing Henrietta's obituary and I need to know what she meant, what the rescue meant, to the community. Do you mind if I record while we talk?"

Dana waved her hand to show she didn't. "I don't know what you'll get for your story. She was always a bit of a recluse. The only person who knew anything about her in recent years was me. Who knows the last time her ex-husband came around to argue with her about something. And then, of course, she fired a volunteer a few years ago. Did you even know you could get fired as a volunteer?"

"What was the volunteer's name?" Sam asked.

Dana shook her head, thinking. The greyhounds

collected around Sam and Pumpernickel. They sniffed Sam's hand and wagged their tails, hoping for pets. Each took a turn to sniff Pumpernickel, the dogs circling around each other, discussing in body language and whisker touches where each had been.

"I don't remember, Sam; she fired so many."

"So she wasn't easy to work for?"

"I'm the only employee who stuck it out. Believe me, we could have used the help. But Henrietta wasn't the best with people. It crossed my mind before about what I would do if she fell ill. We split the work 60/40, but I don't know that one person can do it all. I'm just so behind on getting everything done for the dogs today. Henrietta was really on top of things, and now that she's gone, the rescue is a bit of a mess."

Sam obliged one of the dogs, rubbing a smooth, beautiful, brindle-colored greyhound on its back, the same color as Pumpernickel but a bit smaller in size.

"It looks like you have a real gift with animals. I can see why you're the Pets Reporter," Dana said. "That's Trixie. She doesn't like everyone."

"Like her mother, then?" Sam said. She brushed off the comment about her supposed "gift." The dogs could probably smell the eggs Benedict Sam now realized she'd barely eaten three bites of. "Was there anyone else who might have had a grudge against Henrietta?"

"Henrietta definitely didn't like a lot of people. But in recent years she didn't come across many people in general. And I never saw a dog that didn't love her."

"But you got along with her?"

"Better than others, but that's not saying much,"

Dana laughed and shook her head. "You know, even though she's gone, I can still hear her voice in my head: 'Dana, the latches are done improperly on the cages,' or, 'Dana, it's a miracle these dogs are still alive after the care you've given them.'"

"Wow," Sam said. "Not exactly constructive criticism."

"I loved these dogs, and I couldn't leave them," Dana said, looking at the skinny canines walking around the yard. "If I wasn't here, who else would be? Especially now."

Dana put the dogs first, too, Sam thought. If Dana had had motive to kill Henrietta, she'd certainly made her work hard on herself in the aftermath. Sam grabbed the collar of the large white greyhound as he touched noses with Pumpernickel. Dana directed her to a kennel that said Petey. The two rounded up the other four dogs, who were now calm, and Sam counted eleven in total in their kennels. That meant four of them were running around town.

"Any update?" Dana asked, nodding toward Sam's phone.

Sam checked and read a message aloud: "Four dogs captured and on the way to the rescue." She left out, *Ace reporter, alerting me to this story, Sam!*

"Oh, I'm so glad. Can you help me with these dog beds while we wait? I'm so behind."

Dana grabbed a pile of dirty dog beds, collected in a heap in front of the kennels. There was still the matter of the important document that Henrietta had spoken about, and Sam hoped to sneak away from Dana long enough to find it somewhere in the rescue. Sam reached over to grab a few dog beds as well and wrinkled her nose as the old smell of dog hit her. She jogged a few steps to keep up with Dana, holding her recorder in one hand.

"How long have you been working here?"

"Oh, wow, I guess it would be six years, next January. It doesn't sound like very long, but working for Henrietta, it felt more like 20 years." Dana said she had seen at least two-dozen employees come and go over those years, not to mention all the volunteers and interns, until three years ago when Henrietta had decided to stop her tours, making Dana her only help.

"It wasn't the right decision for the dogs, though," Dana continued, furrowing her brow, as Sam helped her lug dog beds into a supply shed where there was a washing machine, along with bags of wholesale dog food, leashes, collars, and bins of other dog paraphernalia.

"Without the public visibility, donations plummeted," Dana said. "It's been hard to get by, but Henrietta always seemed to find just enough money to buy dog food for another week. Whoever gets this place will have their work cut out for them. Though, I guess, just being nice to people could help the flow of donations."

Dana seemed to pause to consider this, and then started unzipping the cases of the beds and loading them in the washing machine.

"And who does get the rescue?" Sam asked.

"I assume her ex-husband," Dana said. "I haven't heard from him, so I'll just keep taking care of the dogs until someone tells me I can't anymore. And—oh!" Dana slapped her forehead and squeezed her eyes shut tightly, a few wrinkles forming around her forehead. "I have to help my father move into a nursing home in Georgia. My flight is at 9:00 p.m. Thursday night, after the evening feed. Henrietta was allowing me a rare weekend off, but now ..."

She trailed off.

Pumpernickel jumped up on the pile of dirty dog beds, now at least three feet high with both Dana and Sam's contributions. Sam gave Pumpernickel a disapproving look. The greyhound swiftly rolled onto her back, feet in the air, wiggling into bed. Sam looked back at Dana, preparing to circle around the question she really wanted to ask.

"Your flight is after the evening feed? What are your work days like? Your hours, I mean."

"Eight a.m. until six at night, usually."

"You worked yesterday?"

Dana addressed her answer to the washing machine. "Yesterday, I actually left early. I wasn't feeling well."

"Oh, I'm sorry to hear that." Pumpernickel and Sam made eye contact; Pumpernickel still upside down. "So yesterday you just went home?"

Now Dana turned and met Sam's eyes. "Yes, that's exactly what I did. Is that going in the obituary?"

Sam backed off. "I need photos for the story. I noticed Henrietta has a lot of photos in her house. Do you have keys?"

"Oh, no," Dana said. "Henrietta was very cautious about thieves and burglaries. She'd travel a couple of times per year and, of course, didn't trust anyone else—other than me, I guess—to lock the place up properly. I locked up the dog rescue area because she had no other choice, though I suspect that every day after I left, she checked all the locks."

"But—what if you have to go to the bathroom?" Sam asked.

Dana pointed at the back wall. "There's an outhouse behind the shed." She pushed several buttons on the washing machine, smacked it once on top of the lid, and it clattered to life.

"It can be a bit funny," she said.

Sam heard several cars pull up out front of the rescue. She knew the day would get away from her writing all of the dog chase stories, and her time to ask Dana questions was slipping away.

"That must be them!" Dana said.

Dana was the best suspect Sam had at this point, and she wanted to see how she'd react to hearing Henrietta had been murdered.

"Dana—"

But Dana brushed past her out of the shed, running to be reunited with the runaway greyhounds.

"Scooter! Lucky!" Dana called, more greyhound names escaping her as she raced away.

Sam tuned off her recorder. Then she flipped open her notebook and jotted down:

Ex-husband

Mothers' group (dark hair + blonde hair) + green pacifier

Sam realized she'd forgotten to get the names of the women who had reached for the pacifier, either of which could have been Henrietta's mysterious afternoon visitor the day of her murder.

Sam then returned her pen to the page, and jotted down one final suspect's name:

Dana Tripp

CHAPTER SIX

"The obituary can wait, Samantha. We need stories ASAP about those dogs running mad downtown."

Sam sat in the chair in Frank's office again, exactly where she had sat yesterday and become the Pets Reporter. But that felt like lifetimes ago, after all that had happened. After her conversation with Dana ended, Sam had taken a few notes on the greyhound captures, then grabbed a takeaway guacamole panini from Greta's, and had barely taken one bite of it on her way through the door of the *Bugle* office when Frank had called her name.

"Find out what's going to happen to them now that their owner is dead, too. We need a lot of cute pictures." Frank continued. "Of the dogs, I mean."

That Frank could put sentences containing *death* and *cute pictures* next to each other was a testament to his many years as a news editor. A particular kind of distance from the grisly realities of life was necessary. And an eye for any opportunity to get adorable photos of animals or children into the paper.

"I've already interviewed most of the people who caught them, and James was on the scene to get action photos," Sam said, a bit annoyed that she was two steps ahead of Frank and getting blamed for being one behind. "But, there's one thing."

Frank looked at Sam expectantly. Sam took a breath. She wasn't sure how her instincts would be received.

"I know the police are classifying Henrietta's death as an accident until the coroner's report comes back, but I think we should anticipate it coming back as a murder."

Frank laughed. "That's not what I was expecting. I thought you were going to quit! Look, Hodges, this isn't Chicago. This is Birchwood. I'm sorry things won't be as exciting or dramatic here, but when a 65-year-old woman with mobility issues slips in the dark, it's sad, but not grounds for a homicide investigation."

"How did you know it was dark?" Sam shot back.

"I didn't do it, Sam," Frank said, raising his hands in the air, bemused. "Though I guess I have a motive. You saw I was annoyed about her constant phone calls. But, no, I guessed, Sam. It was either light or dark. My odds were 50/50. Get that crime modus operandi out of your head and get me some greyhounds with big, round, sad eyes."

Sam didn't want the conversation to be over yet. "But Henrietta wouldn't stop calling you because she said she had controversial documents she wanted a reporter to see. If someone knew about those, and—"

Frank leaned forward on his elbows, resting them on his desk. His voice had an edge of exasperation. "Hodges, look. Whether or not this was a murder, you're our Pets

Reporter. I'll task our crime department with days of research about whether slippery grass can be a malicious murder weapon. Today, for you, the docket is to get some quotes for our 'Mailman Chases Dog' story, and find out what's happening to those animals!"

The matter was clearly closed.

"I'll get you your stories." Sam grabbed her notebook and closed the door to Frank's office behind her on her way out.

Surveying the newsroom, Sam realized she didn't know where her desk was or if she had even been assigned one. Restaurant critic Yolanda Oliver looked at her from the Lifestyles collection of desks. Her bright yellow cardigan was buttoned all the way up, and an orderly filing system stood perfectly straight next to her pencil cup holder. There was one empty desk next to her. Then Sam saw Tom Albers at the crime desk look up from a phone call and wave to her. His desk was covered in papers, and he furiously shook his pen to draw ink out before giving up and searching underneath the mess for another.

Sam marched in the direction of the crime desk, and as she passed Lifestyles, Yolanda clucked her tongue in disapproval of Sam mixing up the different newspaper sections. Sam would have to remember to bring in a box of strawberry lemon bars from Greta's to smooth things over. She'd read Yolanda's review of Hygge House after it opened years ago and celebrated over the phone with Greta that Yolanda had had *some* nice things to say about, which for Yolanda was the equivalent of jumping for joy. She'd specifically mentioned the lemon bars.

When Tom was done mm-hmm-ing and uh-huh-ing and jotting notes, he put the phone down and stood to hug Sam.

"It's been so long," he said. "You snuck out yesterday, so I didn't get to congratulate you on being the Pets Reporter."

She laughed. "It's been interesting so far. Thanks." Sam remembered Tom's buoyant smile like it was yesterday, realizing the two hadn't caught up in years.

"Where are you off to?" he asked.

"Well, just looking for a desk right now." Sam waved her arm vaguely around the newsroom.

"Sit here!" Tom slapped his hand on the empty desk next to Sam.

"Are you sure?" Sam made an effort not to turn around and glance at Yolanda, who she was sure was watching them.

"Yeah, the crime desk is, well, pretty slow usually." Tom sat down and gestured for Sam to do the same. "It would be nice to have someone else here."

Sam sat down at the empty desk and wiped a line of dust off the surface with her finger.

"Crime does seem very slow," she said, holding up her finger to show Tom. "Hey, do you think Frank created a Pets Reporter position just to get the towns-people off his back?"

"Nah," Tom said. He tried organizing a few of the papers on his desk, but the effect was just a differently-arranged mess. "People do get annoying about pet stories, but I think he's trying to inject a bit of vitality into the

Bugle. I've read your stories; they're always interesting. You'll do great."

Sam regretted that she couldn't return a compliment to Tom; she scanned her brain for one of his stories, but realized she hadn't kept up with news from Birchwood.

"Thanks for the advice," she said, and she meant it. She was glad she'd have a friend in the newsroom. She began to unwrap the guacamole panini.

"Can I ask you for some advice?" Tom said, and lowered his voice.

"Sure." Sam leaned forward.

"Well, you're a crime reporter. Or, you were. Or—" Tom's cheeks reddened a bit, starting to match the brightness of his red hair.

"It's okay," Sam said, taking a bite of panini. She guessed Tom knew the real reason she was back in Birchwood, if he had been following her career from afar. He must have seen the embarrassing videos.

He recovered. "Well, maybe I can just get your opinion. Something about Henrietta's death seems ... off."

Sam paused, the panini held in her hand, frozen in mid-air. "What do you mean?"

"The cop talking to me last night when I called about this kept getting distracted from our conversation, yelling about the lights. I asked him what he was talking about, and he said the backyard flood lights were automatic, so every time the cops stopped moving in the backyard, the crime scene went dark. He was pretty annoyed about it."

Sam listened, taking a small bit of the sandwich.

"But he also mentioned Henrietta had a flashlight. Why would she have that unless the floodlight wasn't working? And it was working fine when the police were there. I feel like someone might have tampered with it."

Sam nodded, encouraging Tom to go on.

"And they said a visitor found the body," Tom continued. "I don't know much about the woman, but I know that she was reclusive and not too fond of people. Why would she have a visitor?"

"I was the visitor," Sam said, to Tom's shock. "But I think you're right. I think she was murdered, too. I noticed the flashlight as well. She had some controversial document she wanted to give me, and I think that factors in. And she did have a real visitor, earlier in the day." Sam explained how she knew, and about the pacifier, and the mothers' group at Hygge House.

Tom listened, his eyes growing wider, and then something seemed to extinguish the light in them. "Okay, but even considering all this, Frank won't entertain it. He always says crime is the slowest desk in the newsroom, and he would know, because he ran it for 25 years."

"Actually, I just told him about my theory," Sam said. "He doesn't want me working on the murder angle, but he did say he'd be happy to have you work on it."

Tom frowned. "Really?"

"Well, he was kidding. But my years of crime reporting have left me oblivious to sarcasm, so if he spots you doing anything related to it, we can say it's my fault. The coroner's report should be back soon, anyway, right?" Sam began pulling out her notebook and pen.

"Norm Felderson is tied up today with a flu outbreak at the retirement home in the next town over, Hanover

Fields," Tom said, flipping around his papers, looking for the story.

"Wait, there's only one coroner for two towns?" Sam put her notebook down, and it released a puff of dust off the desk.

"There's not a lot of death here," Tom explained. "Being surrounded by pets increases health and longevity. Anne DeBraun wrote a really interesting story with some great research about it last week; you should check it out."

In the busy last 24 hours, Sam hadn't even realized she'd have to do some digging into the archives to read how pets had been covered before. That would give her a good excuse to hunt through the archives for information about Henrietta.

"I think her ex-husband might have had something to do with it. Dude's got a temper. I've looked into her family a bit. There's no mention of anyone else around here, just an unidentified relative in New York and a bunch in France." Tom kept rummaging around his papers and then pulled out a photocopied news story.

Sam read the headline: *Man arrested for punching wall at Winters' Autos.*

She scanned the article, reading how Harold Sylvester West had been arrested for destruction of property at Hal Winters'—Greta's dad's—auto body shop.

"Wow," Sam said.

"There's more." Tom handed her a few more clippings: a fight at a now-closed bar in 1983, and another destruction of property when Harold had kicked over a mailbox.

She looked up at Tom. "Well, my guess is someone hit her over the head. I noticed the flashlight, too, so I bet they wanted her submerged in darkness by tampering with the flood lights. My best suspect so far is her only employee, Dana Tripp. But Dana did mention Harold, and said that he and Henrietta argued a lot."

Sam felt someone watching her. She looked around and Yolanda whipped her head back towards her computer so fast Sam worried the top button on her cardigan would pop. Sam turned back to Tom and continued, "She didn't seem very concerned about Henrietta when I talked to her. She happened to go home early yesterday because she felt sick. She didn't look at me when she said it."

"Well, I just got off the phone with Charlie Hume, who lives on Henrietta's block," Tom said. "He said he was walking his malamute, Marty, this morning and Marty went to, you know, and stepped on a shard of glass. Or a shard of plate. It looked like a fancy china plate of some kind, smashed in the grass outside Henrietta's."

"And Charlie called you, and not the police?" Sam continued eating her sandwich.

"He figured it was a public danger the paper could do more about than the cops. No one particularly likes that new guy, Dan Jasper. He's a bit ... abrasive. Especially about pets stuff. So we've been getting extra calls recently."

"Ah, so I've been hired as a backup answering machine service then," Sam said.

"Look, maybe. But we can solve this now, can't we?" Tom's voice was growing louder, more defiant. "Everyone else is dropping the ball on it. This is what journalism is here for. We make sure public servants are doing their jobs." He brought his hand down on a stack of papers, and the messy pile caved in under the weight.

Sports Editor Max Richardson walked behind the crime desk at that moment. He furrowed his brow.

Tom turned in his chair toward Max and held up his hands. "Ah, just discussing crime stuff."

Max said nothing. Sam smiled at him, and he kept walking.

"OK, so if we move forward with this, then, what do you make of the china plate? Pumpernickel had scratches on her legs, too," Sam said, her voice barely above a whisper.

"Who's Pumpernickel?" Tom asked.

"Oh, she's the dog I'm fostering. One of Henrietta's. I think she was there when Henrietta was murdered," She looked around the desk for something to wipe her hands on, and Tom pulled a napkin from the top drawer of his desk and handed it over. Sam nodded in thanks.

"Before we get the dog to an animal psychic communicator, I think we should see if anyone's been pawning some china plates from Henrietta's." Tom's face looked hopeful, and Sam thought he was wondering if she'd partner up with him, if they'd really do this. Their discussion was turning into action. Would she go along with him? A disgraced crime reporter from the big city who'd flamed out too fast, and a small-town crime reporter on an upward, if slower, career trajectory, teaming up to solve a pets-related murder in the pets capital of the U.S.

Sam considered. Based on just the facts, Tom's

suggestion made sense to Sam. If Henrietta had a collection of expensive china, it could be motive enough. If someone needed money—maybe Dana Tripp or Harold West or someone else—it could have been a burglary gone wrong. Or they needed some money and had a vendetta against Henrietta and it was a two-birds-one-stone situation. So far, it was the only lead they had.

Sam considered the obituary. If she would be writing about Henrietta, maybe she could do her own kill-two-birds-with-one-stone. Write a story, solve a murder. She smiled wryly at Tom. *Okay. Here we go,* she thought to herself, putting her sandwich down and diving back into crime.

"So, my bicycle, or yours?"

CHAPTER SEVEN

Tom pulled his car around, a small, dark green hatchback with nicked paint, so that he and Sam could drive to the local reseller. The pawn shop was in a strip mall on the older side of town, the north side. But the new rich from the south liked to frequent Herman's Collectibles & Oddities to find vintage treasures to decorate their large homes.

"I haven't been here since I was 16," Tom said, as he pulled into a parking space.

"I've never been," Sam said. "What have you pawned?" She looked up at the plain, cream-colored concrete building.

"I was always swapping out my video games with Herman. I'd sell ones I'd beaten, buy new ones, beat those, and if there wasn't anything new, buy my old ones back."

"Addict." Sam shook her head.

Tom laughed. "I went cold turkey when I got my first girlfriend."

"Katie Leigh," Sam said. "I remember you guys at prom. Sixties chic, no?"

"My mom still has the photo album to prove it," Tom said, shutting off the ignition. "I didn't think I'd fit through the door with how big my lapels were. Who did you go to prom with again?"

They got out of the car and approached the pawn shop.

"Skipped it," Sam said. "I was finishing the layout of the year's last edition of the *Birchwood High Reader*."

Tom held the door for Sam. "Such dedication."

"Such a nerd, more like." Sam stepped through the entryway.

"You didn't let me finish," Tom said, following behind her. "I was going to say, 'Such dedication for a nerd.'"

He didn't give Sam a chance to reply, calling out as the two approached the counter, "Herman! It's been years. How are ya?"

The collectibles shop was small, but filled with rows of shelving, almost like a used bookstore. On the shelves, however, were VCRs, purses, dishware, and an especially garish cat lamp.

"Tom, right?" said the bald, thin man standing behind the counter. He had glasses on a chain around his neck. "You used to exchange your video games every two weeks. Our inventory took a hit when you stopped showing up."

"My deepest apologies, Herman. My coworker ..." Tom began.

"Sam Hodges, Pets Reporter for the *Bugle*," Sam filled in.

" ... and I have an interest in dishes. Some china plates."

"Something that would be worth it to sell," Sam added.

Herman raised his eyebrows. "Well, 'worth it' depends on how desperate you are in this business."

"I suppose," Sam said, thinking of the rattling washing machine at the rescue.

"Any more details?" Herman said, his hands folded on the counter in front of him.

Sam looked at Tom. "Did, um, did Marty say what kind he was looking for?" Sam thought of the malamute crouched on the lawn.

"Ah, yes, Marty said the particular set he had an interest in was white with royal blue accents, some sort of city or buildings painted on it."

"Ahh, yes, the Duveaux collection," Herman said. "Very nice, from either the late 17th or early 18th century France. Amazing they were passed down that many generations."

Sam and Tom's eyes grew wide.

"They belonged to Henrietta?" Tom asked.

"You know, I'm not supposed to give out customer information." Herman blushed slightly and nodded to a woman standing behind Tom and Sam at the counter. She was short and mousy and waited with a stroller with a small baby to purchase a vintage Jacob's Ladder toy. Sam felt like she knew the woman with shoulder-length, straight blonde hair.

"Hi, sorry to interrupt. Just this," she said meekly.

Herman rang up her purchase and Sam tried to place

her. Tom looked from Sam to the woman, whom she was staring at.

"Are you part of the mothers' group that meets at Hygge House in the early mornings?" Sam asked.

"Yes, I am," she said, seeming a bit surprised.

"Sorry, I just knew I recognized you from there. Sam Hodges, Pets Reporter for the *Birchwood Bugle*. And this is Tom, a crime reporter."

"Clara Wilson," the woman said.

Sam tried to remain cool. She now recognized her. This was one of the mothers who had thought the green pacifier was hers. Sam looked at the baby in the stroller, with his wispy brown hair and waving arms and legs. He had a pacifier in his mouth, one that was exactly the same as the green one, except blue.

"So, reporters? You're writing about the death of Henrietta Duveaux?" Clara accepted her change from Herman.

"No," said Tom, at the same time that Sam replied, "Yes."

They looked at each other.

"Well, we—" Tom said as Sam said,

"No, we were just—"

"Well, good riddance, if you ask me," the woman said, putting her change away in her purse.

"P-Pardon?" Sam said, her voice sticking in her throat.

"She was supporting gambling, a vile vice." Clara nearly spat the words.

Tom let a second pass as Clara handed the Jacob's Ladder to the baby, who grabbed at it with pudgy fingers.

Sam could tell Tom was working something out in his head, but she wasn't sure what.

"And you were personally affected by that?" he said, choosing his words carefully.

Clara's face had softened as she smiled at her son, but Tom's question made it harden again. She looked up at him.

"I used to live on Whisker Street. Now I'm on River Road, and we're needing more space for Rudy every day as he grows. But I can't afford to move back to Whisker Street after my husband gambled all our savings away at that greyhound racetrack"

Sam recognized the different naming styles, and knew that Clara had moved from the wealthy south, most likely significantly downsizing on the north side.

Clara took a deep breath. "That woman was a black mark on Birchwood. We're a wholesome community town, and we don't need her support of gamblers. It would have been better if she'd never started that rescue."

She turned her stroller around, grabbed her receipt off of the counter, and began to leave the shop. Over her shoulder, she said, "Well, I'll let you two figure out if you're working together on that murder story or not."

The bell over the door to the shop tinkled as she left.

Sam and Tom raised their eyebrows at each other, but Herman was looking at them, and they couldn't give too much away.

"So these heirlooms are connected to this murder?" Herman's voice cracked on the word "murder."

"You didn't hear it was a murder from us," Tom said

quickly. He then lowered his voice. "But it would really help us out if you could tell us."

Herman looked side to side, out of the corner of his eyes, as though he were part of a campy spy film. Sam had only ever see people do that in movies.

He cupped his hand around his mouth, leaning forward to say in a low whisper, "It was always an older woman who came in to sell the items. She said they were her family's, and she had a ... a French accent." He drew out the last words.

Sam though of Henrietta's high-pitched voice, her vaguely European accent, and scribbled in her notebook. "Did that same woman come in to sell them on Monday afternoon? We think someone might have sold some ... on her behalf."

Herman looked from Sam to Tom and disappeared into the back room.

"Do you think he's gone to check?" Sam asked.

"That, or he's the murderer and is coming back out here with a blunt, priceless antique object," Tom said.

"Don't be morbid," Sam said, though she appreciated Tom's ability to make her laugh with surprise.

Herman returned with a large, leather-bound book, slamming the heavy tome on the counter with a certain relish, and put on the slim reading glasses that dangled from his neck. "Never did like computers," he said. He traced his finger down his book, and when he reached a line, ran it across. "Henrietta Duveaux, 518 Wichitaw Way. Wait, that's the woman who was found dead, right?"

"Henrietta brought them here Monday?" Sam asked. Henrietta could have pawned them herself.

"Yes, but this was three weeks ago now," he said, flipping more pages. "That was the last time I saw any of those heirlooms. Actually, I think I remember her more clearly now. She had long hair, and a brightly colored shawl."

"She was talking about her dogs, I'm guessing?"

"Ah, yes, that was it!" Herman said excitedly. Despite his previous reluctance, he was now extremely excited about contributing to Tom and Sam's investigation, and Sam figured his earlier reluctance had perhaps been for show. "She came in here every few weeks with a few more of these French pieces. I complimented them, said how lovely they were. She said, 'They'll be more lovely when they turn into dog food for my hounds.' She didn't seem too sad to part with them. Sometimes people are very upset to give away family heirlooms like that."

"So she needed the money for the shelter," Tom surmised.

"Yes, exactly what I was thinking!" Herman said.

"Where else was she getting money from?" Sam asked. If Henrietta had been pawning the pieces herself, it meant their investigation was no longer a robbery-gone-wrong. Now they were also looking for someone Henrietta might have owed money to if she was desperate. Herman looked at them, waiting, and listening intently.

"Thanks, Herman," Tom said, shaking the man's hand. "You've been so helpful today."

"Are you sure you don't have any more questions for me?" Herman asked hopefully.

"Can you let me know if more of those heirlooms turn up?" Sam wrote her phone number down on a blank sheet and ripped it from her notebook, handing it to the pawnshop owner.

Herman took the paper and held it in both hands, like a prized possession. "I'll call you if I come across any clue, any clue at all!"

Sam hoped for Herman's sake that he did find some more clues.

As Tom and Sam began the drive back to the newspaper office, they discussed their new findings.

"Tom, you know what I just thought of?" From the passenger seat, Sam watched the huge oak trees they were passing.

Tom put his free hand to his temple and closed his eyes.

"Watch the road!" Sam shouted, laughing.

"I tried to find out, but you have strong thought-blocking mind control," Tom said, opening his eyes and smiling at her. "I guess you'll have to just tell me in regular old words."

"Clara Wilson talked about the greyhounds coming from a racetrack."

"Do you suspect her as well?"

"I don't think we can rule her out. She was one of the mothers who thought the pacifier was hers, so there's a 50/50 chance she was visiting Henrietta that very day. She has an ax to grind with Henrietta if she blames her for supporting the greyhound racetrack and the gambling problem and all. But, no, I'm thinking about the racetrack. Wouldn't the closest be the one up in Arlington

Park? I even read a *Times* story about the Retired Racer Rescue and it didn't mention where the dogs came from."

"It's called *Retired Racer*, Sam. You don't need a *Times* story to tell you that," Tom said.

"I figured it was a colloquialism. They're fast dogs," Sam shrugged, feeling rusty. An important detail like that, right in front of her, and she'd totally glossed over it. Once again, she was thankful Tom was at her side.

"Well, if Henrietta wasn't naming the racetrack, I'd guess it was the Arlington Park one. If I was getting my dogs from a mafia racetrack, I'd keep my mouth shut about it, too," Tom said.

"That racetrack is owned by the Polini family?" Everyone around Chicago was familiar with the name of the mafia family, some more intimately acquainted with it than others.

"Oh, c'mon, Sam, for sure it is," Tom gave her an incredulous look. "Has Birchwood already made you that soft? Forget about the big city crime family already?"

Sam felt her face go a bit red. First, she'd glossed over Retired Racer and now she didn't even know the Arlington racetrack was owned by the Polini family. She turned to look out the window, at the passing houses, and an old man walking a Labrador puppy.

"Well, we still don't know how Henrietta was killed," Sam said to the window. "So I guess we can't rule out a mafia hit."

"I think it's a possibility," Tom said. "If Henrietta was in financial trouble, her greyhound suppliers would have been more than happy to give her a loan and make sure she kept quiet about how the dogs were treated at the racetrack. They could ensure Henrietta wouldn't talk bad about their greyhound racetrack. You don't want to stir up the animal rights people, that's for sure." The car rumbled as it passed over the railroad tracks, back onto the south side of Birchwood. Tom turned onto Grand Canine Way.

"And she had a controversial document she wanted to give me," Sam said. "If it was outing the Polini family about the dogs' conditions ..." Sam's voice rose an octave. "This all makes sense!"

She whipped out her notebook and began writing. "Okay, crime reporter, you're in charge of checking out this lead. Call up whoever your source is connected to the Polini family, and you don't have to disclose their identity to me." Sam held up her hands wide in defense, smiling at Tom. But her journalism joke hadn't landed. He continued staring straight ahead as he drove, and something had fallen in his face. Sam furrowed her brow.

"Actually," he said. "I don't have any Polini-connected sources. I guess the little *Birchwood Bugle* has never tackled those stories." He looked a bit embarrassed.

"Oh, well, actually, I know someone," Sam said hastily, "So, I'll, uh, just give him a call."

Tom didn't say much the last few blocks of the car ride, and Sam wished for the distraction, as she ruminated over the prospect of needing a favor from her ex-boyfriend at the *Times*.

CHAPTER EIGHT

The next morning at Hygge House, the town was abuzz with the story of the escaped greyhounds. A few general assignment reporters had helped Sam out by jumping on the story, rallying together over the breaking news. It was the same kindred spirit afterward in the newsroom, as they descended on the unassuming *Birchwood Bugle* offices to trade notes and swap stories about getting *the* story. Sam had written furiously on deadline, compiling the notes from the other reporters who helped out.

The cream-colored greyhound that had dived through Dachshund Dad's legs—real name Ted Verner—had eventually been caught by him, though 20 minutes later, and Verner had remarked to the reporter that it was good to get some exercise; he was now thinking about taking up a running routine.

The gray and white greyhounds had run into the train station, where a few baffled commuters had cornered them.

An additional fifth greyhound had never made it downtown, but instead had ended up just three blocks away on River Road, at the Wilson household, coincidentally, where it had dug furiously at the fresh dirt in the front yard's flower garden. Cliff J. Wilson, husband of Clara Wilson, had wrestled the dog to the ground, ruining the white T-shirt he was wearing. He'd expressed triumph over having rescued the dog, though Sam would have liked to get Clara's view on the subject.

The small red greyhound who had wriggled out of George McCarter's hands had been the last to be contained. After escaping George, then a schoolteacher, then the mailman's hands once again, the red dog had finally been caught by a FedEx driver over on Squirrel Street. Sam suspected none of this would be good for the relationship between the U.S. Postal Service and the package delivery service in Birchwood.

And so the stories went that lay spread before Sam in her paper at Hygge House. Sam listened to the gossip for a bit, but no new leads presented themselves, as the town was busy recounting the heroics of the day before. Sam knew she had to get to Henrietta's somehow to find the document.

Greta stopped at her table with a hot pot of coffee in hand. "More?"

"Always," Sam said, extending her cup. "And Greta, hey, who was the mother with the dark wavy hair, the one who lost the pacifier?"

"Oh, um." Greta put her hand on her chin, her face tilting upwards. "Julie, I think. Why?"

"Nothing important," Sam said, waving her hand.

Greta refilled the quick sip of coffee Sam had taken. "Hey, my tenant moving out next week said she'll be gone all morning. You want to have a look at the apartment upstairs?"

"Absolutely," Sam said. She hadn't received a paycheck yet, but the offer was too good to refuse.

Greta handed her a key. "It's number 3A. 3B is an apartment, too, but the rest are hotel rooms. It can get a bit noisy during tourist season but I think you'll like it." She nodded towards Pumpernickel. "Look, Stripey-Pants is even salivating."

"I think it's the bagel I've got here, but I'm salivating over the possibility of not living with my parents," Sam said.

"Great. Let me know what you think." Greta began to walk away but then doubled back.

"And by the way, if you notice anyone acting suspicious by the pastry case, I've been coming up short on croissants in my daily tallies. Some are being made off with. My guess is a toddler with sticky fingers hiding them in his mom's purse, but we'll see."

"I won't trust anyone," Sam said, shifting her eyes back and forth.

"It wasn't me," Mason Reed said from his usual table.

Sam gave Pumpernickel her last bite of cinnamon bagel with strawberry cream cheese, and the two walked through the back of Hygge House to the staircase that led to Hygge Hotel.

Sam had heard once that you should never name your business something people couldn't pronounce, but Greta was obsessed with the Danish concept of hygge, which meant coziness, but in a way English didn't have an equivalent word for. It meant enjoying the simple pleasures, the present moment, family, favorite things, beautiful places. Greta was constantly correcting the customers who erroneously said "Hy-Gee."

"It rhymes with cougar: hou-gah," Greta would say, her voice drifting into a vaguely Scandinavian accent.

Some townspeople had taken to calling it "Cougar Café."

But whatever language it came from, a name meaning coziness was fitting for the café and hotel, as Sam was reminded on the walk up to the apartment. The striped wallpaper around the stairs held ornate picture frames showcasing Birchwood back in the late 1800s, when it had been more known for its livestock veterinary college than stores selling handmade dog tutus.

Sam stopped to look at the sepia-toned photos of Birchwood's ancestors. A man and woman stood, like the famous painting, in front of a small homestead, pitchfork in hand. A couple of dogs were in the background. No tutus.

She wondered if the *Bugle* archives went far enough back that these photos were, in fact, from the newspaper itself. The *Bugle* was a strong record of Birchwood history and life, but Sam had never thought to look how far back it went. She made a mental note, again, to get into the archives as soon as possible to find information about Henrietta. Or maybe the Polini family. Or Harold West.

Sam climbed the rest of the stairs, passed the second

floor full of hotel rooms, and went the rest of the way to the top floor. She unlocked the door and stepped inside.

"Hou-gah, hou-gah." Greta's voice echoed in her mind. How people like Greta could be talented in home décor and baking and cooking and getting along with everyone in town, Sam would never know. She admired it. She herself couldn't cook worth a darn, and her old apartment in Chicago had been more utilitarian than comfort-driven. Her meals as a crime reporter had often been Chinese takeout, and she'd liked to sit on a pillow on the floor in front of her coffee table, her laptop and notebook perched next to her greasy dinner.

Looking around Hygge Hotel apartment 3A, Sam felt all the coziness of returning home, with none of the associated childhood memories or continuing arguments with her parents. She suddenly realized she had no idea how she had lived any other way. This was where she wanted to stay. The dark wood floors were well-trod but all the better for it. In the main room, a kitchenette was filled with big mugs for hot coffee, and a table perfect for two. There were even chairs. Sam smiled.

The adjoining living room had no TV, its sofa facing a giant window, the kind with a little nook and cushion for reading. Sheer curtains were drawn, and the muted sunlight gave the room a warm yellow glow. Pumpernickel jumped on the couch and Sam, a true Birchwood resident, didn't think at all about asking her to get down.

She walked to the nearest wall, a bookcase lined with shelves full of old books, the kind that smelled papery and well-worn. Some were old, some recent years' bestsellers. Sam scanned for the next book in the detective series she had been getting from the town library, and was pleased to see it. Sam knew the rooms in the Hygge Hotel had little placards denoting them as free libraries. Travelers could take what they wanted, as long as they left something in place of what they 'borrowed.'

Sam fingered the spines before walking to the bedroom. It was small, but that was more *test*ament to the expansive bed rather than a diminutive room. Sam closed her eyes and listened. She heard footsteps and soft voices below, probably tourists heading out for a day of shopping or touring the dog park.

Then it was silent. There was no bus brake or automated train announcement. No sirens. No irate yelling outside the convenience store. She suddenly couldn't remember what it was like to be that person she had been in Chicago. Scarfing down unheated Pop-Tarts before rushing to her first crime scene of the night, a workday that began long after sunset. A flurry of tragedy, police, typing. A rotation of endless deadlines that grew closer with each frenzied beat of her heart. And then, an adrenaline crash just as the sun was rising. She'd barely been able to keep her eyes open by the time she got back a few hours after sunrise, the last morning press conference filed away. A quick kiss, like passing ships, with her boyfriend, before he'd leave for his workday with the rest of the world ...

Steve.

Sam opened her eyes and pulled her phone out of her pocket.

She opened her contacts and found the one labeled, "Do not text." Her finger lingered over the contact. She thought of the last day she'd spent in that serviceable apartment with him.

"It's not that big a deal," he told her. "No one cares. You're freaking out."

"I care, and I can react however I'd like. I want you to acknowledge that," Sam said.

"I acknowledge that you care and that you're wrong to care. Besides, even if you don't stay for your career, isn't staying for this enough?" He gestured between them.

Honestly, not at all, Sam remembered thinking. She'd had to break her own heart to leave that job and that city, and yes, even Steve, who hadn't always been such a jerk. She'd had no idea when she walked out of that apartment with her bags packed that she'd be back at a newspaper only six weeks later, as a Pets Reporter.

Henrietta's shawl blowing in the wind flashed across her mind.

She pressed the call button.

The phone rang a few times, and as each tone ended, Sam held her breath, bracing herself. Had he just picked up? He'd see her Caller ID. But then came another ring, and another, until finally a voicemail message clicked on.

"Hi, you've reached Steve Harrison, crime editor at the *Chicago Times* ..."

Sam hung up. She walked back out to the living room and sat next to Pumpernickel, who slowly inched her way across the couch to lean herself again Sam's body.

A ukulele tone broke the silence. Sam quickly pulled her phone back out, but saw Dana Tripp's name on the caller ID.

"Hi, Dana. How are you?"

"Miserable," Dana said. "I'm trying to keep all these dogs fed, but it's taxing. And you still have Pumpernickel, right?"

"Yeah, she's here." Sam rubbed Pumpernickel's head "Do you want me to put her on?"

Sam's humor was lost on Dana.

"No, no, it's okay. Thank you for taking care of her. One less mouth to feed is better over here. These guys seem traumatized."

Sam slapped her head. How had she not thought of it before?

"If you need more foster homes, I can publish a story in the *Bugle* tomorrow, asking for them. Everyone's talking about the escape yesterday, and I'm sure plenty of homes would love another dog."

"Really, Sam? Are you sure? I don't want to be a burden. But if I could get all these dogs into homes by Friday night ..."

"Absolutely. People will be thrilled," Sam said. "By the way, Dana, did you see someone visiting Henrietta Monday afternoon? Maybe a mother with a baby?"

"Oh, that definitely would have been a strange occurrence for Henrietta." Dana's reply was rushed. "But I went home sick anyway, so of course I couldn't have seen anything. Anyway, thanks for the foster article, Sam. Say hi to Pumpernickel for me."

Pumpernickel cocked her head to the side as the call ended and Sam eyed the phone before pocketing it.

"Suspicious, right?" Sam said. "Pumpernickel, if you saw the murder, can you tell me who did it?"

Pumpernickel whined and pawed at Sam's leg. She

rolled onto her back, and Sam obliged by rubbing her belly.

Sam pulled out her notebook and jotted two additions to her list:

Dana Tripp

Ex-husband

Clara Wilson

Polini hit

Sam re-read "Polini hit," sighed, and picked up her phone.

Hi,

It's me. Hoping you could help real quick with a lead. A woman named Henrietta Duveaux was murdered here (possibly) and was getting the dogs for her greyhound rescue from Arlington Racetrack. Did she owe someone money?

Sam couldn't figure out how to sign her name. She added

Hope you're well

And didn't sign her name. Steve would see her email address anyway. She pressed "send."

Sam leaned back into the couch. Her head whirled with the possibilities. She would have to start crossing off suspects soon, as her list seemed only to be growing. If she could just get to that document. Sam resolved to go to Henrietta's that night, and find a way in. But first, she'd head to the *Bugle* to search through its extensive archives.

"Want to make a visit home tonight?" Sam said, rubbing the brindle greyhound, but Pumpernickel was fast asleep, her belly softly rising and falling.

CHAPTER NINE

Sam stood at the top of the stairs that looked down toward the morgue.

"Ready?" a voice said behind her.

Sam turned. James Woods pulled a camera off from around his neck and placed it on the empty desk nearby.

"Yep."

"Morgue" was the industry name for the clippings and old photos kept by the newspaper. For Sam's purposes, the name was fitting, but she hadn't told James their real reason for entering the stacks.

"So we're looking for old photos of the greyhound place, right?" James said, as the two descended the steps.

"Yeah, and if you could also show me how to use the morgue, you know, teach a man to fish and all that," Sam said.

"Of course." James led her down the narrow staircase.

The two planned to go through photos from the archives to choose for Sam's story. Since no one had seen a draft of the obituary yet—much to Frank's chagrin—James had offered that it would be easier for he and Sam to look together, so she could point out the photographs most related to the shape her story was taking. Sam didn't want James to know she was currently preoccupied by a murder investigation, and so her story was taking the shape of accusing everyone who knew Henrietta of having done her in.

In a small office at the bottom of the stairs sat Victor Vine, the keeper of the morgue. When Sam had interned at the paper all those years ago, she had called him the "crypt keeper," and his bony, slender body still fit the bill. Sam and Tom had once giggled over the questions they wanted to ask him that they thought would make good stories—"Local crypt keeper recounts what the dinosaurs were like," "oldest man in the world, only 60 years behind on fashion trends." The two would devolve into laughter before the glowering eye of Yolanda Oliver in her cardigan would shut them up.

Victor's fashion was the same now as it had been then. He sported a purple velvet vest over his collared shirt, and Sam suspected he'd be smoking a pipe if it weren't disallowed in all buildings. The room hummed with the buzz of the fluorescent lights over the rows and rows of filing cabinets.

"Hi, Victor," James said. "We're looking for photos of Henrietta Duveaux for a life story, er, an obituary. When was the rescue started, Sam?"

"She opened it in 1981, ran group tours until 2013." Sam thought back to her employment at the *Times*, with all its digital archives, easily searchable online. The years and years of Birchwood history before her contained a few photos of Henrietta, and possibly some clues to her murderer, but how would she know where to find them? It was a question of a needle in a haystack.

Victor nodded and scratched the information from Sam on his notepad. His writing was methodical, careful. He walked around from behind the window and slowly moved toward the stacks. Sam checked her watch. She had forgotten until that morning that Tammy Trembley's barbeque was that night, Wednesday. Macaroni and Cheese always donned a different elaborate outfit. Sam wondered what famous twosome they'd represent tonight.

Searching through the stacks could take ages. She thought of suggesting to Frank that he should find the resources to digitize the archives. It would take a lot of work, but surely some local research or history interns would be delighted by the task?

Victor took them down to a first stack of filing cabinets and opened a drawer. He ran his fingers over what looked like a thousand stories, all clipped from the *Bugle*, yellowed with age, and pulled out a photo. He handed it behind him as he continued to draw his fingers over the pages.

The photo, showing Henrietta with a gaggle of teenagers, was captioned, saying it was a school trip from the local boarding school, and the teenagers, all girls, ranged in age from 13 to 18. Henrietta looked mostly the same, though her hair was still long, not cut short to her chin, and still black, not gray.

"None of them look too pleased," James said.

Sam scanned their faces: The youngest girl appeared to have been recently crying; the others' somber faces didn't make it look like they were on a field trip.

Sam noticed one girl, next to Henrietta, who was making the exact same face as the Retired Racer owner: stony, like the photo had been taken in the 1800s, when no one smiled for pictures. Their faces drooped, and Sam wondered if Henrietta had the power to pass on her demeanor to those around her. Their black hair had the same slight wave, too. Henrietta wasn't the sunniest woman, and young, troubled girls from a disciplined boarding school probably wouldn't have found the break from the strict school chaperones they'd been hoping for. Maybe that's why the boarding school had chosen Henrietta's for the field trip—she'd have been just as harsh as the teachers. Sam knew Kira Preston, who'd gone to the boarding school, as they both had done weekend volunteer work at the Birchwood Park District together as kids, and she had said it was a strict place.

"I don't know if this is the kind of photo Frank wants for a nice obituary," Sam said. "A bunch of unhappy children."

"We ran it in the paper once before, but I see what you mean," James said.

The next photo Victor handed them with his spindly fingers was from the opening of the sanctuary, in 1981. Henrietta stood proudly in front of a house with the man Sam recognized from his mugshot as Harold West, a greyhound on a leash in front of them. In this one, the young couple was smiling.

Victor produced a photo of Henrietta surrounded by

greyhounds, several eating treats out of her hand, undated. "This will be perfect," James said, excitedly showing her the photo. "Don't you think, Sam?"

Sam agreed, but she was hoping for more photos with obvious clues.

Victor looked up at them. "So you have what you need or you would like to see more?"

"Well, I thought Sam and I could poke around for fun," James said.

"Fun?" Victor said, rolling the word around in his mouth like it was foreign. "All right," he said. He turned and began his methodical walk back to his window.

"Don't you just love how creepy this whole scene is down here?" James asked, his eyes flitting around the stacks, a mischievous smile on his face.

The sound of Victor's footsteps died away. There wasn't a sound besides the faint hum of the lights and Sam could suddenly hear her own breathing. It was eerily intimate.

"Yeah," she said, trying to sound normal.

"And Victor's a trip." James turned around and pulled open a random drawer.

"Tom and I used to call him the crypt keeper," Sam said.

James laughed, his fingers flicking through the files inside. "That's exactly it! But he can certainly find some good stuff. Who even knows how this is organized? If he dies, someone has a large project on their hands."

"I don't think he can die," Sam said. She remembered the death that had brought her down here. "So, hey, how do I find stuff here? Is there a way without Victor's help?"

"Well, from what I've figured out, this stack is the 80s, generally. But then that stack over there seems like it's organized by animal type, maybe? But only since 2000, from what I've seen. It's wild to see all this history. I've never worked at a paper like this before. It's amazing." James stepped one foot to his left and opened another drawer.

"What kind of papers have you worked at?" Sam asked, realizing she didn't know anything about James, except that he wasn't from Birchwood. She opened a filing cabinet next to her and began to look through the photos.

"Mostly just a few different places in LA," James said.

"Oooh, don't let David Yates know," Sam said. "We're still no. 2 behind Paws Palace in LA for the best dog park in the nation."

"Really? I guess I didn't know much about pets when I lived there. There were a ton of Pomeranians in strollers, but I have to say, even Birchwood makes LA look tame," he said. He held up a photo, squinting at it, and then replaced it in the drawer.

"So you were a photographer for the *Los Angeles Times*?" Sam asked.

"No, one of the gossip rags, actually," James said.

Sam stopped rifling through her drawer to look at him. He winked.

"So you're kidding?" Sam asked.

James shook his head. "No, no, I'm really good with faces. They tasked me with finding all the C- and D-list celebrities, you know, the reality stars, people who have gone viral in videos. LA is teeming with them; you just have to know how to spot them."

Sam reddened at the mention of viral videos.

"Aha!" James said. "This is what I love finding." Sam stepped next to him and looked over his shoulder. The photograph he held was of a Golden Retriever, a silver medal hanging around his neck and a birthday hat affixed to his head. The caption read, "Birchwood's Mayor Winston Georges turned five on Saturday. The party was attended by society's best."

He laughed. "See? You always hear about towns that have animals as mayor, but you never really believe it. But here, of course, you guys had an actual dog mayor. Incredible." He shook his head, smiling from ear to ear.

"Here!" James pulled a full newspaper page out of the filing cabinet and unfolded it. It was a full-page photo spread of the mayor's birthday. He read out one caption underneath a woman with a wide, toothy smile: "Breeder Priscilla Clavell announces that Mayor Winston Georges will become a father later this month!"

Sam was still frozen in place, wondering whether James had seen her viral video, since that had been his beat in Los Angeles.

"Why did you leave?" She managed to eke out, finally.

James looked up at her, seeming to remember he was with someone else in the newspaper stacks.

"Oh, LA? Well, after a while, it starts to wear on you. Most of the reality stars can't get enough attention, but sometimes the people who have attracted a lot of attention on social media really just want to live their lives. It's a bit sad, you know? Anyway, do you want to keep look-ing? It's getting kind of hot down here." James returned the photos to their drawer.

It was hot. Sam felt like the walls were pressing in.

"That's why I came here," she whispered. She felt a hotness underneath her eyes, and prayed no tears would fall in front of her new coworker.

"To the morgue?"

"To Birchwood."

"I thought you were from here?" James said. His eyes grew concerned and his brow furrowed. He reached out to pat her on the arm, and then seemed to think better of it. "Sam, are you okay?"

Sam began talking to the floor. "It was a morning press conference. I'd had a string of really long days; I hadn't taken a day off in two weeks. There were three murders. Three! I think I was just exhausted." Sam remembered the dropping feeling in her stomach, the knot that had pulled so tight when she'd realized where she was after her episode.

"But they had me see a shrink afterward. She thought working nights and not seeing a lot of sunlight was a reason, too." Sam remembered the therapist's concerned face, the deep lines around her mouth, her eyes. Profes-sional pressure, the therapist had ruled. But Sam knew there was also the personal pressure, mixing in with the professional. Steve hadn't ever directly mentioned what happened, but talked about it circuitously, as though in code. As though it was unspeakable. Even though he'd said it didn't matter, Sam had known otherwise.

Sam could see that James was concerned about her,

but she couldn't stop herself. She needed someone to know. The stacks were closing in on her. She took a deep breath and barreled full-steam ahead. "I don't really remember it; I must have blacked out. But I just started crying. Like, sobbing. Really loudly. All the TV cameras were there, all the reporters with their phones. The videos were uploaded under anonymous accounts, but it didn't matter who did it. Word spread. Now I'm certain it's going to come back up at the end-of-year 'Reporter Fails' compilations. I'm sure everyone's seen it. I'm sure you have."

In her mind, Sam saw the images of herself on the screen, as though she had leapt out of her skin and was having an out-of-body experience. She couldn't reconcile the two paths her reporting career had taken. There had been the crime reporter, a position at a prestigious paper in the third-largest city in the nation, and then there was the second path, the reporter who was now a meme, an Internet joke.

Sam looked up at James, making eye contact for the first time since he had mentioned his job in LA.

"I haven't, Sam," he said. "I didn't know." He patted her arm.

Sam sniffled. "I'm sorry for telling you all that," she said. But a wave of relief was spreading over her. Maybe she could be both Sams. The former crime reporter who'd embarrassed herself, and now, a Pets Reporter. Maybe she didn't have to be one thing, or be perfect.

James smiled. "Hey, if it were me, I'd want to get it off my chest, too. And I can tell you that there's some new hot viral video every day. People won't care. They won't remember."

Sam smiled too. "Thanks, James."

"And maybe it was for the best! Now you're here, and you've seen what gold we can dig up in these archives. I was sick of the big city. We get obsessed with the national stories, the same thing everyone is talking about. Here, you get to dig up real stories. Real people's lives."

"You're right," Sam said. Somehow, her silly Pets Reporter position was beginning to seem like a better deal than working overnight on crime in the big city. Here, she had a chance to help by solving Henrietta's murder.

Sam held up the photo with the girls from the boarding school.

"Are you okay?" James said, a note of worry in his voice. He must have been concerned she'd devolve into brink-of-tears tirades again about other dark secrets.

"I'm wondering, are any of these girls familiar?" Sam said. "If you're good with faces. Anyone who works with Henrietta doesn't forget the experience, it sounds like. I'm wondering if any are Birchwood residents—"

"For the obituary?" James asked, puzzled.

How could she be so stupid? Sam thought. Sam had confided something she hadn't mentioned to anyone else, but she still didn't want him to know she was trying to solve Henrietta's murder. One admission was enough for today.

"Yeah, well, I'm just having trouble finding sources," Sam hurried to explain.

James took the photo from her, her fingers grazing

hers. He brushed back his auburn hair from his eyes and studied the photo.

"Do you know people in town?" Sam asked.

"I've only been here a year, but I've photographed enough events to pretty much know everyone by face, if not by name," James said, not taking his eyes off the photograph.

"The boarding school is the next town over, I think," Sam said. "Only a few Birchwood girls go there."

"These two know each other," James said. He pointed out a short blonde and the tall, wavy-haired girl with the stony face next to Henrietta.

"Well, they went to boarding school together," Sam said.

"Yeah, but I've photographed them together," he said, scratching his chin. "Oh, yeah! At Mom and Tots swim lessons a few months ago. They both have sons."

"You think they're part of the young mothers' group that meets at Hygge House?" Sam said.

But James was closing his eyes, his mouth moving a bit.

"Jamie ... Jessie ... Jackie ..."

"Julie?" Sam ventured, thinking of the mother who had taken back the green pacifier at Hygge House.

"Yes!" James said, his eyes popping open. He and Sam smiled at each other. "Julie Stanford. Her son is Jean-Jacques, I'm pretty sure." James pursed his lips as he pronounced "Jean-Jacques" in a muddled French accent.

"You're better with faces than accents," Sam teased.

"She was quite insistent about the way I pronounce it. I couldn't spell it for the life of me, either."

"And the other one?" Sam said, gesturing at the blonde in the front row.

"That would be ..."

"Clara Wilson?" Sam said.

"No, Deborah Norwich," James said.

Perfect, Sam thought. That didn't rule out either of the mothers. Julie had a direct tie to the sanctuary, but so did Clara, with her husband's gambling problem.

"Oh, hang on," James said. "You're right."

"I am?" Sam said, grabbing the other end of the photo. They leaned their heads toward each other as James pointed at another blonde girl, in the back row, with a pixie haircut.

"That's Clara Wilson!" James said. "The hair threw me off at first, but you're right, same face."

"Just a guess," Sam said.

Now, Sam thought, time to figure out which of the two mothers had been at Henrietta's the afternoon she was killed.

CHAPTER TEN

"Sam!" Sam's brother-in-law Mark pulled her into a hug. He was stocky and had a huge smile. "And who's this little nugget?" He bent down and Pumpernickel excitedly licked his face.

Sam's sister and her husband were avid pet lovers, and Sam liked to think Frances herself had started the Birchwood pet trend the day she was born. Mark and Frances' two dogs, Miffy, a dachshund, and Boris, a St. Bernard, raced across Tammy Trembley's lawn and began smelling Pumpernickel. Mark initially held them back in case one of them felt threatened, but all three seemed to relax quickly around each other. He let Miffy and Boris go, and the three of them trotted toward the inflatable pool Tammy had set up.

"Sam!" Frances walked over with a veggie burger in hand and gave Sam a big hug as well. Frances was taller than Sam and Mark and usually dressed casually in a T-shirt and jeans, but in a way that seemed effortless and put-together. She had the same hair as Sam, blonde and curly, though Frances' was often pulled back in a bun. "Mom and Dad are looking for you."

"Of course they are," Sam said. Her long days of investigating a murder and working a new beat had left her little time to do anything at home but sleep, and Roselyn had been texting her *"Where are you, Ms. Ghost??"* for days.

"How's the zoo?" Sam asked.

"Oh, same as always, too many politics," Frances said, waving her hand. "But Bernie, the new rhinoceros calf, took his first step the other day! I'll have to show you the video when I'm not focused on food. Seriously, don't let Greta's spread get away from you." She gestured towards the buffet table laden with Midwestern summer favorites: potato salad, coleslaw, corn bread, Greta's signature baked sweet potato chips, and a grill turning out burgers, hot dogs, sausages, and veggie burgers.

"Seriously, get over there quick if you want any potato salad," Frances said, between mouthfuls.

"Gross, Frances," Sam said. "It's not appetizing when I can see it in your mouth." Frances slugged Sam playfully on her arm and held her finger to her lips.

A low bass beat was bumping out of the speakers set up in Tammy's backyard. Adirondack chairs were filled with half of Birchwood, and Sam couldn't guess if there were more dogs or people at the barbecue. With events like this, Tammy made her house on Maple Lane the ultimate hangout for pets and humans in summertime Birchwood.

Mark, who had been play-wrestling with a German shepherd, stood and wiped his hands on his pants. Sam made no hurry to get to the buffet. It was rare that she couldn't eat plenty of Greta's food, even if she wasn't hungry, but she really wasn't hungry after the adrenaline from the morgue earlier that day.

"How's the pets beat, Sam?" Mark asked.

"Well, Henrietta Duveaux, you know, the woman with the greyhound rescue?"

Mark nodded for her to continue as he took a big bite of Frances' veggie burger.

"She was supposed to be my first interview, but I found her, well, dead."

"What! That's crazy."

"Don't talk with your mouth full," Frances chided him.

"She hates it when I do that," Mark said.

Frances smiled at Sam, who rolled her eyes at her sister.

"I think I volunteered there a few times," Frances said. "Can't remember a lot, but I think she was kind of a witch. Not to speak ill of the dead." She made the sign of the cross in front of her.

"Well, I think someone killed her," Sam said, lowering her voice.

"What!" said Mark again.

"Probably," Frances said, taking her veggie burger back out of Mark's hands.

Mark looked at her disapprovingly.

"It wasn't me," she said.

"Who did it, Sam?" Mark asked

Sam liked hanging out with Frances and Mark because she felt like she knew everything necessary, with no subtext between them. Frances had enough going on with the zoo, and Mark commuted into downtown Chicago. With all the animals at their house to take care of, too, (a parrot, a turtle, the two dogs, and two cats) the pair didn't have time for Birchwood's gossip mill. Sam understood why people liked being the one who people came to for gossip. When she had visited from Chicago, Sam had been able to regale them with stories from the crime beat. Now that she was back in Birchwood, they held the same bated breath to hear who Greta had spilled a blueberry smoothie on this week at the Hygge House as she twirled around the café. But this time, Sam had real, juicy news.

"My editor officially doesn't want me following it," Sam said, noting that Max Richardson, sports editor at the *Bugle*, was hovering with a group chatting just a few feet away.

"How could he not? You're a seasoned crime reporter," Mark said, watching someone walking behind Sam. Sam glanced behind her and realized he was probably eyeing the Italian sausage in the man's hands.

"But I never caught the killers," Sam said. "I only wrote about them."

"Well, that makes sense. They probably have real police in Chicago," Mark said.

Frances gave Mark the same play-punch she had given Sam.

"Mark, c'mon," she scolded, looking around her.

"What? I have, to this day, never found my weedwacker, nor one like it."

"I think you lost it," Frances said.

"I know it was stolen, right from under our noses," Mark insisted.

Frances rolled her eyes. "Anyway, Sam, I'm sure I threatened to kill her at least once a day when I volunteered there. I bet you've found a lot of people like that."

"Well, if I take into account every ex-employee, volunteer, or intern, that's dozens of people. And Henrietta pretty much closed the sanctuary to outsiders a few years ago. If someone was going to go postal, I don't think they'd wait years for their feelings to cool off." Sam thought of Julie and Clara. Why would someone want to kill Henrietta now?

"Hmmm," Frances said.

The three of them thought in silence. Mark ate a bite of mashed potatoes off of Frances' plate.

Sam cleared her throat. "Frances, do you think Henrietta's fussiness with her employees could drive someone to murder? Actual murder, not just threats?"

Frances' eyes looked far away. She squinted, the face people made when they were trying to remember something from long ago, as the thoughts bubbled up from the recesses of their brain. "She was very ... particular. She needed everything done her way. In fact, she had these complicated latches all over the rescue. She was very concerned about safety. If you didn't latch them just right, she'd flip. And they were difficult to get undone. I had a full day of training about the latches. Don't even get me started about keeping the dog coats in pristine condition. You'd think they were meant to keep the dogs warm, not glistening like the winners of the Annual Birchwood Dog Show. It's not like I'm—who's that dog breeder—oh yeah, I'm not—" Frances held out her burger with her pinky finger extended. "Priscilla Clavell. Things are much more relaxed at the zoo." Frances shook her head in disbelief. "And we have lions."

Sam thought for a minute.

"I'm also not convinced it wasn't a mafia hit," Sam said.

Mark spat out his mashed potatoes. "I'm sorry?" An Australian shepherd and a Chihuahua were quickly on the scene to clean up the wasted food.

"I don't watch a lot of TV, but do they usually kill little old ladies?" Frances asked.

"Either way, I'm wondering if the dogs know something. When I saw the dogs that night, half of them seemed worked up, pawing and barking at the cage doors. Then half were cowering in the back," Sam said. "They looked afraid. You know animal behavior, Frances."

"Well, were they pawing or cowering when you saw them any other time?"

"No, they were all tail wags when I went back the next day," Sam said.

"So then that's a change in behavior. That's what you have to look for. Our zebra, Razzy, is always kicking up dust for fun. Other zebras only do it when they're mad, but for Razzy, it's normal. It would be strange for her if she wasn't kicking up dust in the afternoons. It's all about a specific animal's behavior."

"I love when you talk behavioral science," Mark said, smiling proudly at his wife.

Sam lowered her voice. "So can animals feel—can they feel guilt?" Sam glanced back at Pumpernickel, who was rearing on her hind legs and pawing at Murray in the inflatable pool. Boris, already tuckered out though he was the biggest of the three dogs, lay in a heap in the grass, watching the other two—and the German shepherd —splash.

"That looks like a happy dog," Mark said.

"We don't know a lot about Pumpernickel's past behavior. Animals are complex," Frances said. "She does look happy, but how does she act when it's just the two of you?"

"She seems skittish sometimes. I brought up the murder earlier today and she whined and pawed at my leg. Of course, she could have just wanted a belly rub."

"So you think Pumpernickel feels guilty about something?"

"You think Pumpernickel is a murderer, Sam?" Mark said, leaning forward conspiratorially.

Sam knew that Mark was kidding, but she wondered. Could Henrietta have tripped over Pumpernickel? Could this all still be an accident? She hoped the coroner's report would come through soon.

Sam spied Henrietta's neighbor, Charlie Hume, walking across the lawn with his malamute, Marty, who had a bandage on his leg, presumably from the broken china plate.

"Oh! It's Henrietta's neighbor. I want to grab him to ask him some questions."

"Okay, reporter, but one thing before you go," Frances said, putting her hand on Sam's shoulder.

Sam continued watching Charlie Hume. "Yeah?"

"If you're feeling crazy living with Mom and Dad, you can always crash with us."

"Yeah, just help with the feeding rounds," Mark said.

"Seriously, Sam, anytime," Frances said.

Sam was still watching Charlie. She tried to pull her arm out of Frances' grip, but Frances held tight. "Sam!" Frances said loudly.

Sam looked at her sister. "He's going to get away!"

"You seem really frazzled by this murder thing. Why don't you come over tonight? Let's watch a movie, unwind. I don't have to be at the zoo until 10:00 tomorrow."

"No, I have plans tonight," Sam said, brushing her sister's hands off of her shoulder. Frances relaxed her grip.

"A date?" Mark asked. He winked at Sam.

"No, I need to find out ..." Sam stopped. "Yes, um, a date."

"Why are you lying, Sam?" Frances asked.

Sam continued searching for Charlie Hume, but he'd been absorbed by the crowd.

"Well, now he's gone," Sam said, her hand falling toward her side.

"You're not going clue hunting in the darkness, are you, Sam?" Frances said, her eyes gleaming.

Sam coughed. "Um, what? No. Why?"

"You're a good reporter but you're a bad liar, Spam," Frances said, using her nickname for her little sister.

"Fine. I'm headed to Henrietta's. She had a controversial document to give me, and I think it has something to do with her murder."

"Do you even know how to break into a home?" Frances said. She gave the rest of her veggie burger to Boris, who had wandered over.

"What?" Sam said, surprised. "Do you?"

"Don't you remember those few months I was in PETA in high school?" Frances said. "They taught me how to break through all kinds of doors. Freeing the animals, replacing meat with tofu, you know, animal rights vandalism stuff."

"You still make me eat tofu. That's crime enough," Mark said.

"I make it taste good. So, Sam, if you're going to go lurking around a murder scene after hours, I'm coming with you. You may be a big-town crime reporter, but you're still my little sister."

"Well, I guess I can't let two women I care about go off into the dark night without the protection of a strapping, strong, and muscular husband—" Mark puffed out his chest and put his hands on his hips.

"Mark, you're afraid of the dark," Frances said.

Mark quickly deflated his chest and held his hands up to show he wouldn't protest. "Then I'll just take the dogs home and get into bed early." He looked relieved.

Sam found Charlie Hume by the dessert bar Greta was setting out, which included her famous caramel rolls, strawberry lemon bar, and a peanut butter chocolate éclair cake. Marty the malamute was nowhere to be found. Probably making friends with the other guests.

"Hey, Mr. Hume," Sam began. Charlie turned around. "I'm Sam Hodges, Pets Reporter for the *Birchwood Bugle*. You called my colleague Tom about the china plates smashed in Henrietta Duveaux's front yard."

"Yeah, my malamute got scratched up by them. You can't have things like that hiding in the grass, not in this neighborhood. Too many sensitive paw pads walking about."

Charlie Hume was in his sixties. Sam had never met him, but she knew he had never married and led a quiet life. Seclusion seemed to suit most of the houses down Wichitaw Way, especially compared to the bustling social lives of those on Sam's parents' Maple Lane. At least Charlie had come out for Tammy's last barbecue of the year.

Charlie picked up a strawberry lemon bar.

"How is Marty doing, by the way?" Sam asked.

"He's fine. It was just a scratch, thankfully."

Sam picked up a plate with a slice of Greta's peanut butter chocolate éclair cake and took a quick bite of the gooey, decadent dessert. But she had to wrap this up to get to Henrietta's soon. The sun was nearly set. Tammy was arranging glowing neon light poles around the backyard and passing around mosquito spray.

"But I meant to call Tom again today," Charlie began. "More of them showed up this afternoon."

Sam nearly choked on her cake. "More plates?"

"Yes, I saw that woman hurrying out with them overstuffed in a brown box this afternoon. When you rush around haphazardly like that, of course some are going to fall and break and pose a danger to the neighborhood."

Sam stared in disbelief. Someone was still taking the family heirlooms from the home, days after the murder. Had they not had time to take them all on the day of Henrietta's death? There was one person who Sam knew was at the sanctuary every day. "Did you know the woman?" Sam asked.

"Nah," Charlie said.

"What did she look like?" Sam said, hopeful.

"My eyesight's not so good," Charlie said. "She looked a bit blurry."

Sam's heart fell, though at least she'd gained some clarity. Her murderer, or at least an accomplice, it seemed, was a woman.

"Thank you, Charlie," Sam said, turning to go.

"Did you come with someone?" Charlie asked.

Sam turned back with a look of disbelief on her face. Was Charlie asking if she'd brought a date to the barbecue?

Charlie pointed to Marty, who had reappeared and was poking his head out from under the dessert table. "He's mine."

"Oh," Sam said, relaxing. "Yes, I have a greyhound. Or, I'm fostering a greyhound named Pumpernickel." Sam suddenly realized she hadn't seen Pumpernickel in the crowd for a good hour. The dog was usually by her side, and though it had only been for a few days, she felt uneasy. She turned from her left to her right, and suddenly didn't recognize any faces, human or animal in the crowd. It was the feeling again coming over her—not being able to place where she was. Chicago? Birchwood? A press conference?

A black cloud seemed to be forming around the edges of her vision, and her head began to feel light. She felt the empty plate drop out of her hand and grabbed onto the edge of the picnic table to steady herself. She wished she could feel Pumpernickel's smooth fur under her fingers, a small comfort that grounded her in place.

"I have to go find her," Sam said to Charlie, her voice shaking. She bent down to pick up the paper plate and deposit it in a garbage bag then raced away from the dessert table and into the chattering crowd.

CHAPTER ELEVEN

The neon lights of Tammy's mosquito torches pulsed and glowed with the rumbling sound of the bass beat. Sam couldn't be sure if they were flickering or she was imagining it. As she passed by groups of Birchwood residents, she looked into their faces, hoping to see a familiar one, but people just eyed her as she walked by. She looked from their faces down to their feet, but the dogs underfoot weren't Pumpernickel. She scanned as she walked, not sure which direction she was going. The night enveloped her like it used to in Chicago, but this time, she didn't feel at home in the darkness.

A hand fell on Sam's shoulder, and she started. She turned to see Clara Wilson holding a glass of red punch.

"Samantha, right?" Clara said.

Sam nodded. "I'm looking for Pumpernickel. One of the greyhounds."

"Oh, let me help you," Clara said. She stood, as if waiting for instruction from Sam. When Sam didn't make a move, Clara asked, "Where did you last see her?"

"Over by the pool, playing with Miffy and Boris," Sam said. A cool breeze broke the hot summer night, and the fresh air and conversation cleared her head a bit. Her heartrate subsided.

"Let's go check over there. Walk with me," Clara said. Sam fell into step next to Clara, and Sam could see from the corner of her eye that Clara opened her mouth and then closed it a few times.

"Was there something you wanted to tell me?" Sam asked.

Clara swallowed, and looked Sam in the eye. She took a gulp of her red punch.

"I think I got a little too, um, feisty at the pawnshop the other day—" Clara nearly tripped and looked down. Macaroni and Cheese were circling Sam and Clara's feet.

Sam laughed. They were dressed as Sonny and Cher. Macaroni sported a black wig, and Cheese wore a blue blazer that reminded Sam of Tom's prom outfit. Clara scooped up Cheese in her arms, setting her empty punch glass on a nearby cooler, and Sam picked up Macaroni.

"I got you, babe," Clara sing-songed. Sam groaned at the corniness of Clara's joke, and Clara giggled. "Sorry, that was so bad," she said. "I'm going to blame it on Greta's punch."

Sam giggled, too, and looked into Macaroni's big brown eyes. She couldn't stop laughing at the dog's tiny face enveloped in the ridiculous wig. Sam suddenly felt that she liked Clara. Perhaps Clara had just caught her at the right time, helping to turn the unfamiliar, dark backyard into a warm, dog-filled gathering of friends.

The two fell into step again towards the pool, still carrying the tiny dogs.

"The other day," Clara said, breaking the comfortable silence after a minute. "I realize I came off as, well, a bit bitter."

Sam stopped, knowing it was best to see Clara's face while she told her this. Sam really hoped Clara wasn't a murderer, but she couldn't let that get in the way of things now. Clara's face glowed in the orange light. Dramatic shadows fell across everyone's faces at the party. Off in the corner near the pool, now, it was darker than it had been near the dessert table. Sam couldn't even make out anyone else. They were just silhouettes.

"Cliff hasn't been to the gambling race track since Rudy was born, but I've become more protective since then. I didn't realize it. I hadn't thought about Henrietta or that gambling racetrack in years, Sam, and it brought up a lot of old feelings. Our house is smaller now, but it's okay. We'll manage." Clara's eyes pleaded. She seemed to be seeking some sort of absolution from Sam. When Sam didn't respond, Clara continued, "I just feel so bad, speaking about her like that. It's terrible what happened to her."

"It's okay, Clara," Sam finally said. "I know you didn't kill her." If Clara hadn't thought about Henrietta in years, that meant she hadn't been over at her house to drop a pacifier earlier that afternoon.

"I—I just know that you and Tom are investigating it, and I figured I looked pretty guilty."

Macaroni yipped at something across the lawn, and

Sam let her down. Clara released Cheese as well. She stood back up.

Sam put a hand on Clara's shoulder. "Just don't let people know we're looking into it," Sam said.

Clara nodded. "I won't, Sam, I promise. You know, I know the mother's group can be a bit cliquish, and I really would love to talk about something other than Rudy. So next time you're at the café, would you want to have lunch together? Or just a coffee? Or whatever," Clara said.

"Sure, Clara," Sam said. She imagined the two of them giggling over coffee at Greta's, and very much hoped now that Clara wasn't a murderer. And she didn't want Clara to be offended that Sam couldn't just take her word for it. A trick Sam had picked up in Chicago was blaming anything that could alienate a source on a faceless editor. Steve had encouraged it: "Whenever you have to ask for something you don't want to, just blame it on me."

Now, she had Tom as her scapegoat.

"Listen, Clara, I believe you, but Tom won't be as easily convinced," Sam said. She waited to gauge a reaction, but couldn't tell from the flickering light disguising Clara's face. "Could you tell me, for his sake, where you were between 6:00 and 7:00 p.m. on Monday?"

"I was ... just at home with Cliff and Rudy," she said.

"Anyone else who would know that?" Sam asked.

"I phoned my mom. I'm sure the phone records could show that, right? Can you get those?"

Sam couldn't, not without a warrant and the help of

the police, but if Clara was bluffing, she didn't want her to know.

"Yeah, that's no problem," Sam said, not wanting to lie to Clara. She really didn't want to lie to anyone. It was just stretching the truth. Sam had police sources in Chicago who could do favors for her, and she could get them if she needed to. But it would be a bit of a hassle, and Clara didn't seem as promising of a lead as she once had.

"Thanks, Sam," Clara said, pulling Sam into a hug. Maybe it was Greta's punch again. Sam hugged her back and checked her watch; she really wanted to get to Henrietta's before it got too late. And she still hadn't found Pumpernickel.

"Sorry, I've been blathering away," Clara said. "Wait, is that her?" Clara grabbed Sam's arm and pointed toward a corner of the lawn about 30 feet away, even darker than where the two women stood.

Sam saw the shape of a dog nearly like a skeleton in the shadows: spindly legs, long snout, whiptail. "That's her, or another greyhound," Sam said as the two approached quickly.

A man was bent on his knee, petting Pumpernickel and talking to her.

"Pumpernickel?" Sam said. Sam's eyes adjusted to the darkness, and the dog barked once and tried to pull away from the man, who kept her firmly in his grasp.

"This is your dog?" he said incredulously. Sam had expected a deep, gravelly voice, but the man sounded young, almost like a teenager.

"Clayton?" Clara asked. Sam and Clara were now

just feet from the dog and the man, and Sam worried something bad was about to happen.

But the man stood and said, "Yeah?"

"It's Clara. Wilson, now," she said.

"Oh, hi, Clara." A bright light shone on the man's face. Sam turned to see one of the party guests climbing a tree, attempting to put a spotlight in it, as Tammy directed him with shouts from below. Sam turned back. The man's face was a bit pudgy, and his sandy hair was matted with sweat. He wore a navy-blue polo shirt, khaki shorts, and boat shoes.

"This is your dog?" he said, still holding onto Pumpernickel's collar. Pumpernickel whined, and looked at Sam.

"I'm a cat person," Clara said, and Sam nearly gasped. It was a controversial thing for Birchwood. "It's Sam's dog. Sam Hodges, Clayton Clavell. Clayton, Sam."

"Hi," Sam said. "You can release her now. Thanks for finding her." Clayton let go and Pumpernickel dove in between Sam's legs, where Sam could feel that she was shivering slightly.

"Clayton and I went to school together," Clara said. Sam figured Clara was around 30, which would have made her just old enough that the two never would have crossed paths at Birchwood High.

"Uh, yeah," Clayton said, his eyes darting back and forth between the two.

"Your family breeds dogs, right?" Clara said. "Honestly, my nightmare. Though I guess breeding cats might actually be worse."

Sam was thankful that Clara was chatty with the

punch and in high spirits after being apparently absolved of her murder charge. There was something off about Clayton, and Sam wanted to be able to study him without worrying about filling the silence. He was sweaty, but perhaps it was just the summer heat. This September in Birchwood had been brutally hot, nearly record-breaking. His ill-fitting polo looked like it was years old, but the designer label meant it had cost several hundred dollars. And why had he been so interested in Pumpernickel? He hadn't been talking to anyone, he'd just been over here, in the corner, with Sam's dog. Sam got a jolt of adrenaline, and thought of Clara saying she had become more protective since having Rudy.

Sam hadn't heard what Clara had been saying, but she looked at Sam as if she had just asked her a question.

"Sorry, what?" Sam said.

"I thought maybe you could do a story on Clayton's family, as, you know, the Pets Reporter," Clara said. "A long line of dog breeders—I'm sure there's something interesting there. Clayton, give her your number so she can follow up."

Sam recognized that Clara wanted to help out her new friend, but Sam didn't want to do a story on Clayton's family. He was giving her the creeps.

Clayton fumbled with his wallet, a nice leather that had been tattered by being overstuffed. He dug through the many business cards, scraps of paper and bills to find a card, which he extended to Sam.

"Clavell Enterprises," Sam read. The card was heavy cream paper, the type on it formal and plain. "Vice President."

"It's my dad's business," Clayton said. "We hire cars for executives across the suburbs. Airport transport. Commuting downtown. That sort of thing. The dog breeding is just a side hobby, really. It's nothing important. Something to keep my mother busy."

"Right," Sam said. "Well, I better be going with Pumpernickel."

"So soon?" Clara said.

"Just catching up on work," Sam said. She had a funny feeling about leaving Clara alone with Clayton. "Walk me out and let's set up a coffee date, Clara. Nice to meet you, Clayton."

Clara and Sam turned and left, and Pumpernickel kept close by Sam's legs as they walked, pressing her body ever so slightly against Sam's knee. Sam didn't want to turn around to confirm it, but she felt Clayton's eyes watching them walk away.

CHAPTER TWELVE

"So what are we looking for?" Frances whispered. Sam and Frances were sitting in Frances' parked truck, a dirty Ford pickup that had seen better days but was perfect for driving down the unpaved Wichitaw Way street on Frances' way to the zoo. Sam had directed Frances to Henrietta's, and they'd parked a block away. Pumpernickel was in the back, lying on a mess of blankets, old uniforms, and other laundry.

Sam sat in the passenger seat. "Henrietta mentioned some explosive document; it was why I was doing the story about her in the first place. I have a feeling that has something to do with her murder."

"Like a report or something? An exposé?" Frances whispered again.

"If someone wanted that information to stay hidden, they could have killed her for it," Sam said. "And you don't need to whisper."

"Let's go," Frances said. They got out of the car and walked down the block towards Henrietta's. As they got to Henrietta's front lawn, Sam pointed her thumb, and they turned up the walkway. Frances slunk like a burglar, taking wide, soft steps on her toes.

"You're going to attract more attention walking like that than walking normally," Sam pointed out.

"I'm the expert," Frances said. "I've got all night anyway. Remember, I work late tomorrow."

"Well, let's try to make it quick," Sam said as they arrived at Henrietta's front door. They didn't want to risk entering through the back and drawing the attention of the dogs.

Frances slid her credit card against the door lock, a trick Sam was certain only worked in movies. In reality, Sam had heard it only served to help any would-be burglars stop racking up credit card debt by cutting up their cards. But the knob turned easily when Frances tried it.

"That's amazing," Sam said.

"I didn't think it would actually work," Frances said. "Actually," she pushed on the door. "I think it may already have been unlocked."

The two stepped slowly inside. The house was dark, and eerily quiet.

"I'll go upstairs," Frances whispered.

"We're the only ones here," Sam said, in a normal tone of voice.

"Shh, you're the worst criminal in the history of criminals," Frances said, throwing her hood over her head. She had insisted she and Sam both change into the dark-colored hoodies she had stashed in the back of her truck, which they'd pulled out from underneath Pumpernickel, who seemed exhausted from the party. Sam's hoodie smelled like the bat house at the zoo. She had to breathe through her mouth to keep from coughing.

"I'll check down here," Sam said, breaking away from Frances to enter the living room. The empty house didn't feel like a gravesite or a crime scene, but Henrietta had been murdered here, Sam was sure of it. It could have been whomever she'd met with earlier that day, which now seemed to be Julie, and not Clara. It could have been her ex-husband in a rage. It could have been a disgruntled employee. And for some reason, Sam now suspected it could have been Clayton Clavell, too.

Or, perhaps, whomever the document held damning information about.

Sam walked into the living room, the mausoleum of the hundreds of greyhound photos. There were two display hutches with dozens of frames of dogs. Sam thought to look for the origin of the heirlooms while she was there. There wasn't a spare surface in the living room. Perhaps Henrietta kept them in storage?

Sam walked closer to inspect the dog photos. She shined her phone light on them, again seeing more dog names across the bottom of each frame: Patches, Ricardo, Ella. Some photos featured what must have been volunteers or employees from when Henrietta still allowed them at the rescue. One photo showed a young, slim woman with a wide, toothy smile. Sam thought she recognized her from somewhere.

But her focus was pulled away when she heard a small crash from upstairs, like something had been dropped or knocked over. *Oh, Frances,* she thought, shaking her head.

As Sam turned her light back to the case, she noticed an area where a picture frame had been knocked forward. She picked it up and it showed a dog named Molly, an aging greyhound who might have been black in her younger days, but was showing gray hairs around her muzzle in the image.

The hutches were dusty, but Sam noticed that behind the photo was a ring empty of dust. In the center of the ring, the dark wood of the shelf glistened. Whatever was once there—a china bowl, perhaps?—had been removed recently. Sam shone her light down the rest of the case and saw many more dust marks of heirlooms that had been removed from behind the dog photos. It would have taken some time to remove them, as a swift job would have knocked over all the pictures.

From what Sam could see, only Molly's frame was lying down. The murderer might not have had time, the night Henrietta was killed. If she'd been murdered during the evening feed, sometime between 6:00 and 6:30 p.m., Sam arriving just before 7:00 could have disturbed their heist. But they'd come back. Charlie had said it was a woman. Could she be in cahoots with someone else?

Satisfied with a piece of the heirloom puzzle, Sam turned her attention to finding where Henrietta might keep an important document. Her attention was drawn by a closet she hadn't noticed before, tucked away in the corner of the living room.

As Sam got closer, she realized the closet was huge.

She pulled aside the drape covering the entrance. It turned out it wasn't so much a walk-in once you got inside, as it was filled to the brim with many big tubs and containers. She opened the lid of one and saw dozens of dog collars inside. Another revealed bottles of vitamins. The third was full of manila folders, and her heart started beating faster.

She flicked her fingers over the files, putting her phone in her mouth to have both hands free. She passed labels reading "Yearly check-ups," "Change of address," and "Washing machine warranty." Sam stopped on a folder labeled "Bills" and pulled it out.

There were receipts and bills inside, in a jumble of papers. There were outstanding payments owed to Percy Harris, the vet, as well as Grayson's Dog Food Supply, but no records relating to the racetrack. Sam rifled back through the tub, not finding any folders with labels that might show any connection to Arlington—or the Polini family.

A sudden siren made Sam freeze. Then she recognized the sound as a dog howl a second later, and her spine tingled as she relaxed her muscles.

Sam knelt down on the carpet, thinking. She flipped up the lids of the nearby containers and pulled open a few drawers, but it seemed the only one with paperwork was the tub she'd already gone through.

She passed over the documents in the tub again, this time more slowly. She found a manila folder that wasn't labeled, which she'd missed the first time. When she pulled it up, however, she realized it was labeled, just low enough that you couldn't see it when it was filed away.

The label read: "Urgent!"

"Bingo," Sam said, and her phone toppled out of her mouth, falling onto the floor with the light facing upward, right into Sam's eyes.

"Ugh," Sam said, squinting. She picked up the phone in one hand and pulled out the folder with her other hand. A large brown envelope peeked out of the folder.

"Don't move," said a man's voice behind her.

CHAPTER THIRTEEN

Her legs shaking, Sam slowly stood and turned to face the entry to the closet. A man appearing to be in his 50s stood in front of her, his silver hair just visible from her phone light. As Sam held the light down by her side, it was shining upwards, giving him a spooky glow, lit from underneath, as though he was about to tell a campfire story.

But the scary story was real: he was pointing a gun at her. Sam, for once, recognized a face from a younger photo. The man looked a bit older than he had in the newspaper: It was Harold West, Henrietta's ex-husband. Sam thought of James, and how he might be proud she had recognized a face. Sam grew angry at herself, annoyed that she was thinking about James when here she was, perhaps about never to see him or anyone else ever again.

Sam said nothing; her voice seemed to be caught in her throat. What was Harold doing here? Why did he have a gun? Why was he pointing it at her?

"Mr. ... Mr. West," she said, defaulting to what came most naturally to her—asking questions. "Why do you have a gun?" she whispered the last word, as though it was too dangerous even to say aloud.

"In case of intruders like yourself. Breaking and entering." He didn't stop pointing it at her.

Sam thought of what she knew of Harold and his violent past. "But this is Henrietta's house." In her shock, Sam was actually confused, but her question must have come off as a threat.

"Oh, so I'm breaking and entering then, too, you're saying? Who do you think the police will believe when I call them? Her legal husband, who was just checking on the property, especially after some vandal came and cut a hole in the fence, and then found an intruder? Or someone dressed up like a cat burglar, snooping around my ex-wife's house?"

Sam regretted letting Frances dress her up. Wait. Frances. What was that thump she had heard from upstairs? Had Harold already gotten to Frances?

"What do you have there?" Harold's eyes flashed down to the envelope in Sam's hands.

"Henrietta had some documents to give me, but unfortunately, she was—she died before she could give them to me. It was important to her." Sam gripped the folder tightly.

"Well, since I'm her husband and helped pay for the down payment on this house, I would say those documents actually belong to me." He smiled wickedly as he held out his hand and began walking toward her, the gun down by his side. Did Harold know what the documents were? Would they be bad for him, should they be released? Had Harold murdered Henrietta?

"No," Sam said. She squeezed even harder on the envelope, and felt her fingers might fall off, but it was better than handing it over to Harold. "Actually, they don't belong to you."

Harold was now standing in the small closet with Sam, and she could smell cigarette smoke on him. Closer, now, his face was unshaven, and his eyes looked wild. Sam's heart pounded.

She slowly raised the envelope and held it in front of her. Harold looked down at it.

On the front, written in permanent marker, was *"For Samantha Hodges."*

Sam cleared her throat.

"Sam Hodges," Sam said, her voice growing stronger. "Pets Reporter for the *Birchwood Bugle*. I don't think we've met."

Sam powerwalked out of Henrietta's house. Harold had agreed to let her go without calling the police, but watched her from the porch. Sam tried to stop herself from running as she went down the block to where they had parked the car. She whipped out her phone and texted Frances:

Ex-husb inside! Get out!

Sam could pull the car around the block and try to get into Henrietta's from the backyard, but if Harold came upon her a second time, would he shoot her? And why was he at Henrietta's house? Looking for clues? Covering his tracks?

Sam's phone beeped:

In the car

Sam ran the last 20 feet to the car and opened the door. Frances was sitting in the driver's seat, and Sam threw her arms around her.

"I heard a man's voice downstairs but overheard you sounding like you had it under control. So I climbed out of her bedroom window."

Sam pulled out of the embrace to look at her sister. "What? How did you climb?"

"I landed in some bushes; it's fine."

Sam picked a leaf off of Frances' head. "You are definitely out of practice, Ms. Animal Rights Activist," Sam said.

"We're both safe, and it looks like you've got some secret documents." Frances pointed to the papers in Sam's hand. "So I'll say that we did pretty well for ourselves."

"And that thump I heard?"

Frances shrugged. "I dropped a box I was trying to get off the shelf in Henrietta's upstairs closet."

"Smooth. Maybe that's what Harold heard, too."

"But I found a copy of Henrietta's will." Frances smiled, waving a brown envelope in front of her that looked similar to Sam's. Sam's eyes grew wide. Maybe her sister was more of an asset than she'd thought.

"Let's get out of here first, though," Frances said. "Getaway driver's orders." She peeled the car out with a screech, and Sam rolled her eyes. If breaking and entering was one of Frances' skills, subtlety wasn't.

Frances drove Sam back to her and Mark's house, also down Wichitaw Way, though closer to the zoo than downtown Birchwood.

Frances had told Roselyn that Sam would be staying over for movies that night, and Mark had driven back in a separate car with Boris and Miffy.

As soon as Frances and Sam walked through the door, Mark made a fuss over his wife's scrapes from the bushes she had landed in.

"Just be thankful she didn't break her leg," Sam said.

"Let's open these suckers up!" Frances said, grabbing the brown folder from Sam.

"I'll make you some tea," Mark said, disappearing into the kitchen.

Sam and Frances sat on the couch. Boris, Miffy, and Pumpernickel crowded around, too, feeding off the obvious anticipation of the humans as Frances ripped open the envelope and pulled out a single sheet of paper. As they turned it over, Frances read aloud, "1st Annual Dog Zumba Show of Skills at Birchwood Community Gym, Sunday, September 18th, dogs and spectators' pet welcome. Tickets $5 each, all proceeds go to Retired Racer Rescue."

"Sam," Frances said.

The two of them stared at the flyer, and at the tacky

clipart of a dog and a woman doing the salsa that made up the center of it.

Mark sat down and grabbed the flyer. His eyes scanned it.

"Well, Sam, either someone has gone through all the trouble of stealing your document and replacing it with a bogus one, or that little old lady just wanted to get some newspaper coverage of her Dog Zumba exercise class."

Sam flipped over the paper and found tiny handwriting in pen on the back.

"*Sam—I did not approve this event and do NOT approve of Dog Zumba. Very cruel for the animals. – Henrietta.*"

Sam's face fell, and she felt embarrassed in front of her sister and her brother-in-law. She had been talking to them all night at the barbecue about the murder of Henrietta Duveaux and some secret, explosive documents. She was trying to solve a murder as a reporter, as though she had any experience actually solving crime. Instead, she was making a fool of herself at her new job. And she had, tonight, nearly gotten herself and Frances killed.

Mark put his hand on Sam's shoulder. "You okay, Sam?"

She looked up at him and frowned. "I put us in danger tonight just to get a Dog Zumba flyer." Sam felt on the verge of tears, or laughter, possibly. "Maybe I'm all wrong about this murder. It is Birchwood, after all, not Chicago."

Frances laughed and patted her younger sister's shoulder.

"Sam, Mark and I may not be smack in the middle of the gossip mill of Birchwood, but even we know that it's not to be messed with. People may sound like they're gossiping about who painted their dog's nails an ugly color, whose lawn hasn't been mowed, or—"

"Or the infamous weedwacker thief, still on the loose," Mark chimed in.

"Or that," Frances agreed. "But we all know that everyone in this town has secret jealousies, they hold onto grudges, and they love to stir the pot."

"You might find more out at this Dog Zumba class than you think," Mark said, picking up the flyer. "Maybe it's a clue."

Sam took a deep breath and looked at the flyer, trying to withhold judgment.

"If whoever is running Dog Zumba is trying to raise money for Henrietta's rescue, and Henrietta was trying to stop the fundraiser, that's kind of strange," Sam said.

"She must really hate Dog Zumba," Frances said. Then she jumped up from the couch and raced into the kitchen. Sam and Mark exchanged confused looks. Frances returned a minute later with a white and green booklet and handed it to Sam.

"The community rec center class schedule," Frances beamed.

Sam flipped the pages in the book until she came to one with "Pet-Friendly Group Exercise Classes" as the title. She ran her finger down the listings, marveling at Dog and Human Swim Lessons, Dog Soccer, and, of course, Frisbee, with five different subgenres of Frisbee classes.

Sam found the listing for Dog Zumba and saw that over the summer the classes were Tuesdays and Thursdays from 9:00 a.m. to 10:00 a.m. She read the listing aloud.

"Perfect!" Frances said. "Just show up tomorrow for a drop-in."

"I think I will," Sam said. She looked at the instructor's name: Summer Salander. Sam couldn't puzzle out why anyone would be so against Dog Zumba as to not accept charitable proceeds from it. Obviously, the sanctuary had money problems. Dog Zumba sounded silly, sure, but Sam still couldn't believe that this was the controversial document Henrietta had wanted her to have. But, after all, she hadn't known Henrietta, had, in fact, never met her, and had to piece together what she knew about her after her death.

"And the will?" Sam said, nodding at the folder lying on the couch next to Frances.

"Oh! Almost forgot, geez," Frances said. She pulled the folder over and unwound the red string that held the top in place. As she worked, the room was quiet except for the snoring of Boris and the thump of a mug as Mark finished his tea and placed the ceramic cup bearing the words "#1 Zookeeper" on the table.

Frances pulled out the slim stack of documents and placed them on her knees, while Mark and Sam, on either side of her, leaned in to read over her shoulders.

"The Retired Racer Rescue is going to Dana!" Sam exclaimed.

"It was changed a week before the murder," Frances noted, pointing to the date in the top left corner.

"And it's not just the rescue," Mark chimed in. "Look, it's everything at Henrietta's address, 518 Wichitaw Way."

"Who are we giving all our earthly possessions away to in case of catastrophe?" Frances said, turning to Mark.

"I think we put Boris in charge," Mark said. Boris's snore stopped for a moment, then resumed when he didn't hear his name again.

Frances stretched her arms above her head and let out a loud yawn.

"Why are you yawning?" Mark said. "I have to be at work at 8:00, and Sam has Dog Zumba at 9:00. You don't have to go in until 10:00 tomorrow."

"But that means I'll be doing evening cleanup, and that's a heck of a lot harder than morning prep. We all need our sleep." She turned to Sam. "I don't know if I'll make it through a movie."

Sam waved her hand. "Frances, don't worry. I just want to go through this will with a fine-toothed comb."

Sam carried the empty teacups into the kitchen, comfortable at her sister and brother-in-law's house, and Pumpernickel jumped up from where she'd been and followed. Sam called goodnight to Frances and Mark, and climbed the stairs. Like the rest of the house, the guest bedroom felt more modern than either Roselyn or Henrietta's home, and also the apartment at Hygge House. Frances and Mark had built the house just a few years ago.

A pair of gray sweatpants and a bright teal shirt bearing the words, "Birchwood High Science Club" waited on the bed, and Sam changed out of the floral dress she had been in for the barbecue. She'd have to stop by home or borrow Frances' clothes the next day, before setting out for the community center in the morning.

Sam padded across the carpet to the connected bathroom and found a new toothbrush and a small tube of toothpaste waiting for her. As she brushed, she thought over the events of her long day. There had been the confrontation with Harold. She thought about all the anticipation she'd had leading up to the reveal of the controversial document, and how she was certain it would be an airtight murder motive that sent her investigation in one direction with certainty. But if Harold had even suspected Henrietta had worrisome documents about him, he wouldn't have let Sam leave with that envelope, whether her name was on them or not.

Sam had been looking into the white porcelain sink, but then looked up at her reflection. She hadn't had a lot of time for noticing her looks the past few days, but saw suddenly that her face looked better than it had in Chicago. Maybe it was the terrible lighting in her small studio in the city, but she looked healthier here. Her face was fuller, her skin brighter. Her hair wasn't as greasy.

Pumpernickel was already curled up on the edge of the bed, and Sam pulled back the covers. Her mind still churned over everything she knew about Henrietta. Everything had felt like it was over when the document wasn't a doctored financial report, or a revealing letter from an angry associate—the type of documents that would make any reporter's day in Chicago. But Frances and Mark were right. Wasn't a Zumba poster the equivalent in Birchwood?

Sam slipped into bed, ready for a good night of rest. She'd wake tomorrow with renewed determination and energy to find out what was going on with Henrietta Duveaux, and who had killed her.

Sam propped herself up on her elbow and slipped the charger for her phone into the wall. She picked up her phone to check her email. She hesitated for a second, sighing deeply, knowing that it would be full of messages from residents with stories, press releases from every pet business in town, and probably a few emails from Frank, assigning her stories and asking about the obituary. She had slipped in and out of the office that day without seeing him, and if he knew how much time she was spending on her "obituary," he certainly wouldn't be pleased. Sam had relished the absence of emails during the last month and a half, as her email inbox had ballooned to more than 100,000 unread messages during her stint at the *Chicago Times*.

Sam felt something pressing on her feet. She looked up to see Pumpernickel was standing, looking at her. Sam held her gaze for a second, and then said, "Pumpernickel, we have to solve Henrietta's murder, okay?"

Pumpernickel sighed, turned three times in a circle, and then lay down again in a ball.

Sam clicked on her phone. She had two missed calls from Tom, which she hadn't expected. As a reporter, Sam's phone was always on, but she'd forgotten she turned it on silent when she and Frances were breaking in to Henrietta's.

Sam looked at the time: 11:00 p.m. She didn't want to call Tom back, knowing he worked the crime desk beginning at 8:00 a.m., so she went to her email. There were 88 new emails—not bad, but she scanned quickly through the list, until she came upon one from Tom.

It was a forwarded email, and Tom had added only, "Here we go."

The email was a report from Norm Felderson, coroner for Birchwood and Hanover Fields. He had completed his analysis of Henrietta's cause of death and concluded it was a "traumatic injury to the head." No word of whether that was an accidental fall or something else. What was Tom getting at? There wasn't a lot of information here.

Sam scrolled through the rest of her emails. There was one from John Lowe, following up on the squirrel explosion on Westward Avenue. Sam opened it and the email was only pictures she guessed John had taken. There were images of Westward, and Sam had to admit, if you looked closely, there certainly were a lot of squirrels in the trees.

The last photo was blurry, as though it had been zoomed in past the point of clarity on the camera. It was an old woman holding something out to a squirrel, and Sam recognized the blurry red box in her hand: Ritz.

Sam giggled a little, and then louder, until Pumpernickel raised her head and looked back at her as if to say, "I'm trying to sleep."

"Sorry," Sam said, covering her mouth with her hand. "Squirrel humor. Dogs might not get it." Pumpernickel put her head back down.

Sam scrolled through more emails. A press release from Danielle's Every Day Dog Wear, which would be revealing its new fall line at the end of the month. Another press release from the local birders association with data from the migratory birds they had tracked in the spring. And more emails. And more.

Sam's eyelids began to close, and she knew it would be better to let the rest of the emails wait.

But then—another forwarded email from Tom. She hadn't seen it the first time she'd been hunting for his name.

It was a press release from the police.

For immediate release from the Birchwood Police Department:

The death of Henrietta Duvueax,65, on Sept. 4, has been reclassified as a homicide.

Investigators found a golf club covered in blood at a residence in the 4800 block of River Road, and both occupants have been brought in for questioning.

Tests have been sent out to determine a DNA match of the victim with the new evidence.

If you have any tips related to this crime, please call 555-0101

Sam's thoughts whirred. Police were officially classifying Henrietta's death as a murder.

A bloodied golf club had been dug up in someone's yard on the block where Clara Wilson lived.

CHAPTER FOURTEEN

Sam entered the community center dressed in a pair of jeans and a faded green T-shirt that Frances had lent her. Sam had snoozed her alarm three times, choosing extra sleep over a morning bike ride all the way back to her parents' place on Maple Lane. Now that she was dressed in Frances' old clothes, she was feeling a bit frumpy (her sister was at least four inches taller than her and much broader-shouldered as well) and wishing she had made the trek. Sam tied up the T-shirt in an attempt to look more put-together. She wondered what animal secretions the shirt had seen and shuddered, quickly deciding not to wonder anymore.

The community center was a huge gray warehouse-like building, and Sam could already hear faint barking from the parking lot. Sam knew that the coldness of the exterior of the building hid the treasures that were inside: an Olympic-sized swimming pool and hot tub, a rock-climbing wall, volleyball courts, every exercise machine known to man, and that was just the start of it.

Sam and Pumpernickel pushed through the doors and walked up to the welcome desk, where Sam recognized Colleen Heath. Sam wondered for a second how far apart in grades they were, as they had never crossed paths in Birchwood's school system, but as soon as Colleen opened her mouth to reveal a slight Southern drawl, Sam knew she hadn't grown up in Birchwood.

"How can I help you?" Colleen asked, her name badge displayed over a fleece jacket imprinted with the logo of the Rec Center.

"Could you point me in the direction of the Dog Zumba class?" Sam said. She gestured at Pumpernickel, who stepped forward to match Sam's position in front of the counter. "I'd just like to see it."

"What do you mean by 'see'?" Colleen asked, narrowing her eyes.

"Well, I'm Sam Hodges, Pets Reporter." Sam had hoped she'd be able to sail through easily, but now she flashed her business card. "And I just wanted to ask Summer Salander—"

"Nope, sorry, Ms. Hodges," Colleen said, shaking her head. "We don't allow people to just watch the class. We've had trouble in the past with people posting videos on social media. Apparently, some people find the idea of Dog Zumba to be a little bit *funny*. So we no longer allow anyone not participating in the dance class to be admitted."

Pumpernickel jumped up so her front paws were on the counter. "Oh, hello!" Colleen smiled and opened a jar of dog biscuits, passing one into Pumpernickel's mouth.

"But if I participated ...?" Sam ventured.

"If you both participated." Colleen's eyes lit up. "You want a monthly pass with canine companion to the Rec Center?"

A gaggle of young, college-aged girls streamed into the center behind Sam and each gave Colleen her membership card. She swiped them through.

"Enjoy, ladies!" she called as the chattering troupe, dressed in volleyball gear, kept walking.

"Just a day pass," Sam said.

"We only offer monthly," Colleen said.

"Okay," Sam acquiesced. Maybe she and Pumpernickel would be checking out five different kinds of Frisbee. "But I'd like a receipt." She needed to ask Frank about work expense procedure at the *Bugle*.

With a newly-printed membership card in hand, which included a picture of her and Pumpernickel, Sam made her way to the Dog Zumba class. She skipped the locker room Colleen had pointed out, not having anything to change into, and knowing it was the perfect excuse to just watch the class, as opposed to participating. Colleen had gotten her to pay, but she wouldn't get her to dance.

In Studio 4, Sam peered through the window in the door to see a woman with blonde hair—with pink streaks —sashaying and spinning in front of the mirror. The woman was wearing a reflective silver bodysuit and a bright pink sweatband to keep her hair out of her face. A black lab wearing a flower crown lay nearby, biting in between its paw pads.

Sam pushed the door open, and could hear the

woman muttering under her breath, "One, two, three, four ..."

Sam cleared her throat.

"Oh!" the woman said, spinning around to look at her. She looked Sam up and down, frowning at her baggy jeans and shirt. "New to Dog Zumba?" she smiled.

"Hi, yes," Sam said. Pumpernickel clicked behind her, her nails sounding on the spotless hardwood floor. "Summer Salander?"

"Yes, that's me. You'll want to change right quick; the class is starting soon."

"I actually just wanted to speak to you—" Sam began.

"I've got to firm up these moves before class, I'm sorry. We've only got a few weeks before our fundraiser show, and I just haven't been sleeping since Monday," Summer said.

Sam's ears perked up, "Since Monday?"

"Let's speak after class," Summer said sharply, her hands on her hips. Sam could tell she wanted Sam out of her waist-length hair.

"I'm not dancing, just—"

"No spectators," Summer said.

Sam looked down at Pumpernickel, who looked up at Sam and wagged her tail excitedly.

A few older women opened the door, chattering just like the volleyball players, and streamed into the room. They were all wearing different spandex outfits, similar to Summer's. A dachshund, Golden Retriever, and yellow Lab trailed them, also sporting a bit of flair.

"I don't have anything to wear," Sam said.

"Well, why didn't you say so?" Summer said. She

trotted to her gym bag and came back, handing over a piece of navy blue material with stars. "And for the lady," Summer said, extending an extra flower crown and looking down at Pumpernickel.

Sam did her best to force a smile.

In the women's locker room she had initially skipped over, Sam stripped off Frances' jeans and T-shirt, and stretched the navy blue spandex suit over her. Pumpernickel did her feet-lift dance, anticipating the Zumba class.

"Henrietta didn't like Dog Zumba," Sam whispered to her as she affixed the flower crown to Pumpernickel's head. Red roses. Pumpernickel raised her head as if proud of her new adornment. "But you don't seem to mind," Sam said.

Sam heard Henrietta's name from around the corner of lockers, and stopped moving. Had the women heard her? But no, they were in the middle of their own conversation.

"Her ex-husband has been prancing around town with a *younger woman*," a voice said.

"He has certainly *grieved*, hasn't he?" another scoffed.

"Well, they were divorced," a third voice said. Sam, who had knelt down to put the flowers on Pumpernickel, began inching her way toward the voices on her hands and knees.

"Me and Arnie have been divorced 25 years, and I

still would respect the man for a week were he to bite the dust in an unfortunate accident," the first voice said.

"You've threatened to kill Arnie more times than I can count, Betty," the third voice said again.

"Well," the second voice interjected. "If you ask me, I think it's the same situation here."

"What do you mean, Doris?"

"I think he killed her!" Doris said, and the other two women gasped. "They weren't *divorced*, Phyllis. They were separated. Henrietta wouldn't sign the papers when he wanted to marry that pretty young thing from Canada a decade ago, and the girl didn't stick around long after *that!*"

"It was in the *Bugle* this morning that the police are now classifying it as a homicide," Betty's voice said.

"I thought things had a bad foreshadowing when she didn't take his last name. A marriage like that is never going to work out," Phyllis said.

Sam had inched her way to the edge of the lockers, hoping to see the three women and figure out which one was Doris, the one with the murder suspicion.

"Oh, we have to get going," Phyllis said, and Sam heard them walking toward where she was crouched.

They turned the corner, and the three of them eyed her on the ground.

"Can't find my earring," Sam said, smiling, patting her hands around the floor. Pumpernickel barked.

The three women shrugged and kept walking.

Sam grabbed the purple gym bag Summer had lent her and hurried out of the locker room and back into Studio 4.

As she opened the door, she spotted a woman in neon pink leggings and a white t-shirt with "Zumba con Perro" spray-painted across the front.

"Glitter for everybody!" she shrieked, dumping a handful into Sam's blonde hair. Sam instinctively closed her eyes as the sparkles rained down.

About thirty women with 30 dogs all stood chatting excitedly. Sam overheard snippets of conversation:

"If you really want to flatter your curves, you just have to go with black ..."

"I can't find a flower crown big enough for Georgine's head ..."

"I've almost learned every word in *Despacito* ..."

Sam hurried with Pumpernickel to the front of the class. Her phone chimed with a text message and she looked down. There was a new message from Clara.

"Sam, it's not ours. Please believe me!" the text read, and Sam knew she was talking about the golf club. She wasn't sure what to believe. After she got some information from Summer Salander, and hopefully whoever the mysterious Doris was, she would rush back to the newsroom to conference with Tom about the developments.

Sam heard a ukulele song and at first whipped her head around to see if class was starting. She then realized it was coming from her phone.

The Caller ID said, "Do not text." Sam blew out the breath she realized she was holding, and picked up the call.

"Hi," she said.

"Sam!" Steve said, his voice high and chipper.

"How are you?" The conversation felt forced and

formal, but Sam knew it was her fault. When was the last time she and Steve had spoken?

"Busy. I'll tell you that. We have a private sit-down with the mayor at noon today, and it was unexpected, so we're scrambling to figure out what angle we want to take and which reporter to send. We've only got 15 minutes...."

In her mind, Sam pictured Winston Georges, Birchwood's dog mayor from the *Bugle* archives, and a young *Chicago Times* reporter, sitting down opposite him with a notebook and pen, eagerly awaiting the chance to ask him some hard-hitting questions about a new train line development.

But of course, the real mayor of Chicago was not a Golden Retriever.

"... and then we'll have to figure out where to budget it in the print edition, but anyway. That's just another day in the news, right?" Steve said, breaking Sam's reverie. "What are you up to, Sam?"

Sam looked at herself in the mirror, wearing the full bodysuit covered in sparkly stars, as silver and purple glitter speckles floated down from her hair onto her face and arms. Pumpernickel wagged her tail, looking up at Sam, her whole body shaking from the force.

"Two-minute warning!" Summer Salander called from where she was fiddling with the stereo system.

"Um, just writing boring stories at my desk. Another day in the news." She turned from the mirror to a blank wall, to be able to focus and pretend she really was sitting at a desk, working on a story to rival a sit-down with the mayor. "Did you get my email?" she asked.

"I checked out your mafia lead," Steve said.

"And?" Sam's voice caught in her throat. She hoped she wasn't about to get tangled in a mafia story that was dangerous to report, but was the only other option Dog Zumba?

"The family didn't have it out for Henrietta. They wouldn't have killed her."

Sam breathed a sigh of relief. She could rule out one suspect, finally. She thought of Dana inheriting the rescue, of the murder weapon being found at Clara's, of what she had newly learned about the violent Harold West, his separation from Henrietta, and his new, young girlfriend.

"But," Steve said.

Sam gulped. "Yes?"

"Henrietta was selling some of the champion racers at top dollar to breeders. The racetrack owners didn't mind, but those dogs were quite valuable to the right people."

Sam suddenly thought of Winston Georges again, but she shook the image out of her mind. The tip confirmed Sam's initial hunch that Henrietta's secrets ran deep. Not everything in Birchwood was as it appeared. How could Henrietta be selling the dogs, when she was claiming outwardly to be a rescue, a nonprofit? If she had been desperate for money, it made sense though. *Desperate people do desperate things*, Sam thought.

"Wow. Okay, thanks, Steve. Look, I've got to run. Breaking news, you know," Sam said.

"I heard you're the Pets Reporter over there," Steve said, and Sam could hear a smile in his voice.

"Yeah, well, um," Sam dropped her phone, and the impact shut it off. She groaned. She had made a fool of herself. But he wasn't her boyfriend anymore. She didn't work at the *Chicago Times*. She wasn't living in Chicago.

Pumpernickel nuzzled Sam's hand with her nose, and Sam turned to face her new home, its crazy residents, and their beloved furry friends.

"Ready?" Summer chirped from the front of the room, a microphone headset around her head. A saucy Latin beat pulsed from the speakers. "Five, six, seven, eight!'

CHAPTER FIFTEEN

The beat thumped as Sam tried to keep up with the complicated moves all the other ladies seemed quite practiced in. Pumpernickel wasn't faring much better, as it seemed all the other pooches were quite adept as well. But the greyhound didn't seem to mind; she delighted in running circles around Sam, trotting on her four feet and barking along with the human claps Summer Salander instructed.

Glitter fluttered down past Sam's peripheral vision with every twirl and spin. During the fifth or sixth song, Sam started to get into the salsa rhythm, and began to feel a bit cocky about her newfound Zumba skills. Once she caught a look at herself in the mirror, however, she once again fell behind the curve. The stars and the jumpsuit weren't helping.

The eighth song was a partner dance, and the ladies paired up, Sam quickly weaved through the crowd until she overheard a voice that sounded like Doris.

"Excuse me," she asked Doris' partner. "I think my

greyhound has a crush on this little schnauzer. Do you mind us cutting in?"

As if on cue, Pumpernickel excitedly sniffed the schnauzer and then promptly rolled onto her back on the ground to entice him to play.

Doris' partner, whom Sam recognized as either Betty or Phyllis from the locker room, moved off to find someone else.

"Doris," the gray-haired woman said, smiling down at the dogs. "And this is Orion." Orion had been charmed, as he was now running circles around Pumpernickel. The way to a woman's heart in Birchwood was definitely through her dog.

As the music picked up, and Summer directed a beginning hip bump to the beat, Sam whispered, "Sam Hodges, Pets Reporter for the *Bugle*. I'm actually writing about Henrietta Duveaux."

Doris' penciled-in eyebrows arched.

"Grab your partner's hands!" Summer yelled.

Sam grabbed onto Doris' spindly fingers, and the two fell into step.

Sam was better at dancing, she noticed, when she was trying furiously to concentrate on something else.

"I knew her husband many years ago," Doris said, her eyes shifting from side to side. "We ran in the same circles around Birchwood."

"Harold seems like he ran in some wild circles," Sam said, thinking of his violent tendencies and his frequent bar fights.

"We were younger then," Doris said, and her eyes

crinkled around the sides. Despite the furious shaking of her hips she was doing, she seemed a bit sad.

Summer clapped her hands twice, meaning the dancers had to switch which partner was leading.

"But now, the circles he runs in, they're ... younger?" Sam said, cocking her head to the side and arching her eyebrows a bit.

Doris nodded, and Sam spun her. They fell back into step.

"He's been seen around town with one of the women from the mothers' group," Doris said.

"Clara?" Sam gasped. She said it too loudly, as Summer glanced back at Doris and Sam and gave them a disapproving glare.

"I don't know," Doris said.

Summer instructed the dancers to pick up their dogs, if they could. A short woman with a bob in the front picked up the front two paws of her Great Dane, but a woman next to her, who clearly had been frequenting the weight-lifting classes at the Rec Center, heaved her heavyset Chocolate Lab into her arms as he squirmed.

Sam scooped up Pumpernickel, though her arms burned under the weight—was Pumpernickel heavier than she remembered? Doris picked up Orion. They sashayed their hips from side to side, facing the front of the room.

"She has black hair," Doris said out of the side of her mouth. "Very tall and slim."

"She's a Birchwood resident?" Sam asked. She thought of Julie.

"She moved here about five years ago, I think from New York. No husband in tow."

"So the baby ..."

Doris shrugged. She mouthed, "Harold?"

Pumpernickel struggled from Sam's grasp and landed on the hardwood floor on all fours.

"Okay, switch partners!" Summer yelled, and a woman next to Sam let down her Chihuahua and grabbed Sam's hands.

Summer Salander disappeared as soon as the class was finished. Sam hurried to the locker room showers, eager to change and stalk the halls for the Zumba instructor.

Feeling the warm spray on her skin, Sam thought over what she had learned at Zumba class. Harold was seeing a younger woman, and she had a year-old baby in tow now. Maybe she'd wanted to make things official, and Harold had been willing to do away with his difficult ex-wife to get it done.

As for Summer Salander, Henrietta certainly had a bone to pick with Dog Zumba, but what was her platform? Clearly, there were dozens of women in Birchwood who loved the class and their peppy teacher. Would one old woman's complaint really threaten Summer's livelihood? Perhaps Summer had forgotten that Sam wanted to speak to her. Sam didn't know whether to suspect her or imagine she had a packed class schedule. *Wait,* thought Sam, *the schedule. Of course!*

Sam rummaged around in her backpack and pulled

out the green and white Rec Center booklet Frances had given her the night before. She searched through all the dog classes and found that Summer also taught one of the Frisbee classes—"Dog Frisbee Dance," of course—as well as Dog Yoga and Dog Tai Chi.

Sam looked at the days and times. *Bingo,* she thought.

Dog Tai Chi was Monday and Wednesday evenings from 5:30 to 7:00 p.m. If Summer had been teaching a class Monday night, then she couldn't have killed Henrietta.

On her way out the door, Sam stopped to talk to Colleen again.

"How was class?" Colleen said, smiling, looking up from her desk.

"Great," Sam said, a little out of breath from having run down the hallway. "Colleen, I wanted to try Dog Tai Chi, too."

"Your monthly pass includes all of our classes!" Colleen said brightly.

"Great!" Sam said. "You know, Summer was just great as an instructor."

"Everyone loves Summer," Colleen said. "And you're in luck. She teaches Dog Tai Chi on Mondays and Wednesdays."

"But does she ever have substitute teachers?" Sam asked, suddenly worried.

"Oh, no, never," Colleen said.

"So last week, for instance, she taught both the Monday and Wednesday?" Sam asked.

"Yep," Colleen said. "I worked both nights, and she

was here. She gets to her classes early to make sure her routines are flawless."

"Awesome." Sam's face widened into a grin. One suspect down. The documents were found. And she'd ruled out the person they pointed to. She felt one step closer to solving Henrietta's murder, and hoped Tom would have more leads and more details about the golf club. Sam was certain they were getting closer.

CHAPTER SIXTEEN

S am had Pumpernickel with her, but only hesitated for a fraction of a second before deciding that as the Pets Reporter, if anyone could have a dog in the newsroom, it would be her. Thankfully, as she walked by reception, Wendy cooed over the greyhound so much that Sam offered to let her babysit Pumpernickel at her desk. Wendy was ecstatic.

As she passed through the doors into the newsroom, Tom raised his head and caught her eye. Sam waved and picked up her pace to trot over to him. Yolanda Davis, wearing a light purple cardigan, showed horror on her face as Sam walked by. But this time, Sam was prepared. She'd stopped by Hygge House on her way to the newsroom.

"Yolanda," she said, reaching into her messenger bag and pulling out a small white box with blue ribbon around it. "These are for you. I thought you liked them."

Yolanda put on an exaggerated face of confusion. She

opened the box slowly, as though certain it would contain a bomb.

"Oh!" she squeaked when she saw them: powdery and glistening, red and yellow, soft and buoyant strawberry lemon bars.

"Thank you," Yolanda said, and Sam could tell she was trying to hide a smile as she placed the box on her desk.

"No problem," Sam said, as she walked over to the pod of crime desks.

Sam tried to stifle her wide smile as well. Winning over Yolanda had been easy. Why hadn't she thought of bringing her lemon bars as an intern? Sam slung her bag onto her desk and looked at Tom.

"Tom, I—"

"Hodges!" came a gruff voice from the back of the newsroom. Frank was standing outside his office, wearing a short-sleeved, checkered, green-collared shirt. The chattering of the newsroom came to a stop as everyone turned to look at Sam. Sam smiled at Frank, wondering if Pumpernickel was a problem, and walked through the newsroom to his office. Once she began moving, the tension was cut and the chattering picked back up. Frank motioned Sam inside.

Frank closed the door and sat down behind his desk. He ran his hand over his head. "So, Henrietta Duveaux was murdered."

Sam waited.

"You were right, Sam. What do you think of that?"

Sam's expression curled into a frown. What did she think of it? This was another of Frank's strange tests.

"Well, I guess I have good instincts from being a crime reporter."

"And now, what's your position?" Frank

"Pets Reporter," Sam said. Ah, so that was where Frank was going.

"So, as Pets Reporter, you haven't been running around town trying to hunt down suspects, now, have you?"

Sam shook her head.

"Sources tell me differently," Frank said, and he leaned forward on the desk.

"What sources?" Sam shot back, wondering who had been talking to Frank about her. Her question betrayed her guilt, and she regretted it the moment it came out of her mouth. Frank smiled, knowing she was caught.

"A newspaperman doesn't reveal his sources," he said. "From now on, if you'd like to stay Pets Reporter, I'd like you to pre-approve your stories with me. Send me what you'll be working on by 9:00 a.m., and then check in at the end of the day with any stories you have finished. Got it?"

Sam felt like a child in the principal's office.

"Yes, sir," she said.

"Great," Frank said. "What have you been working on today?"

"A Dog Zumba story," Sam said, suddenly realizing there was a bit of glitter still falling out of her hair onto her hands.

"Dog Zumba? That's phenomenal," Frank said, laughing. "I knew you'd make this beat your own, Sam. Get me that story by the end of the day. Any photos?"

"No, I had to, well ... participate," Sam said.

"I'll send James the next time it's on," Frank said, scanning down his calendar. Sam prayed she wouldn't be roped into another session the same day that James would be there. Part of her quite liked Dog Zumba, but the other part of her didn't want anyone to know that fact.

"Tuesday," Sam said, and Frank nodded and penciled it in.

"Well, Sam, I look forward to reading that story later today," Frank said.

Sam hesitated. She hadn't talked to anyone in an official sense, and Summer and Colleen had seemed so intent on not letting visitors in. Sam was very relieved that Summer hadn't killed Henrietta, because if she was upset about anyone threatening her Dog Zumba class, Sam was about to do it, by writing a story that might attract unwanted attention. The women had a good thing going, a secret, safe community, and she didn't want them laughed at online. Sam knew all too well how that felt.

"I didn't really get usable interviews," Sam said.

"No problem. Do it in the first person," Frank said, and his phone rang. He waved Sam out of the office as he took the call. "Martin!" he barked. Sam groaned. Write the story in first person? Now she'd bear the brunt of the criticism, if any, on the Dog Zumba story.

Sam stood outside Frank's office and dug into her bag for Henrietta's secret document. The flyer for the Dog Zumba show in a few weeks was the perfect news hook for her Dog Zumba report, whether she liked it or not. She was trying desperately to solve Henrietta's murder, and so far, the deceased woman had helped her keep her job.

"Thanks, Henrietta," she murmured to herself.

Sports editor Max Richardson walked by, looking at her curiously.

"Just Pets stuff," Sam said, smiling innocently.

Sam noticed Tom's hand waving in the air behind Max, and excused herself. She hurried to the crime desk and sat down.

Tom wheeled his chair close to the corner where their desks met.

"Did you get my emails last night?" he said.

"Yes," Sam said.

"What happened to you?" Tom said, his eyes drifting up to her hair and then down to her ratty, too-large T-shirt.

"Dog Zumba," Sam said, waving away his confusion. "I'll tell you about it, but listen, I think Harold did it. I've got some new info."

"New info from breaking into the guy's house?"

"What? I don't even know where he—" Sam sat back in shock, until she realized that Tom was referring to her break-in of Henrietta's house. "How did you—"

"Harold called Frank and said he wouldn't alert the police, that he just wanted Frank to know what you were up to in your off-hours. He said you even introduced yourself as a reporter for the *Bugle* while committing the felony."

"That's not how it happened," Sam said, growing hot around her neck. So did the whole newsroom know? She imagined what she must look like, coming into the newsroom well past 11:00 a.m., no one knowing what story she had gone to cover that morning, covered in glitter and wearing baggy clothes. Not to mention the breaking and entering.

"Sam, listen, since Henrietta's murder is now official, let's let the police do their job," Tom said. "I know it's disappointing for both of us."

"Disappointing?" Sam shot back. "How is it disappointing?"

"That's the wrong word," Tom said, and he looked down at a paper on his desk. He crumpled it up and pushed it away, his cheeks now beginning to grow red.

"What's that?" Sam said. She grabbed for the paper and Tom tried to stop her, but she picked it up, stood up, and stepped away from his reach. Tom looked around the newsroom.

Sam read the paper silently in her head: "Notice: Retirement party for Paul Cornhull, Friday Sept. 29. Hiring: crime editor. Please alert Frank to your interest."

"So," Sam said, looking up at Tom. "You were hoping solving a murder might boost you to the front of the line for crime editor here? And now that Frank is upset about me, you want to fall back in line to get the job that way?"

Tom grimaced. "Sam," he said, his voice soft. "I just thought it might be better if you sat in Features ..."

Sam was shocked. Tom had been so happy to help her out, offer her a desk, and have fun staking out the Pawn Shop with her. And now she was a pariah in the newsroom?

Sam said nothing as she put the notice about the

crime editor position on Tom's desk and grabbed her bag. But she noticed there was a white envelope on her desk.

"What's this?" she asked Tom.

Tom held her gaze. "James left it for you."

Sam reddened. She put the envelope in her bag and walked over toward Yolanda Oliver and her purple cardigan.

"Hi," Sam said, smiling and knowing it looked fake since she was silently fuming.

"Hello," Yolanda said, her icy demeanor having returned. She coughed and went back to staring at her computer screen, though she pushed the box of strawberry lemon tarts closer to Sam. Sam picked one up and shoved the whole thing in her mouth, letting the sugar release its calming, dopamine effects in her brain.

Sam had expected seeing some of this behavior when she'd slunk back to Birchwood, that she wouldn't be readily accepted by the town. That people would think she thought she was too good for the small suburb, too important to be a small-town reporter, or even just a small-town resident. She had never been in love with animals, and that was sure to be another point against her.

Then there was her viral video. Sure, everyone in town had their secrets, but none were going on a national stage and embarrassing the town they had come from. The secrets were local, and private, and a part of Birchwood. Sam had gone and embarrassed herself in the big city. Maybe everyone thought she deserved it.

But when Sam had arrived in Birchwood, everyone had been so friendly and so willing to help her out. It was through her own doing that she now felt alone. Sam fired off an email to Frank that she needed to return to the Rec Center to confirm a few details about a few other dog exercise classes. She picked up her bag, and knew what would make her feel warm, welcome, and cozy. After all, it was right in the name: Hygge House.

CHAPTER SEVENTEEN

S am could always count on Greta to make her feel
better. Well, Greta herself, and a healthy dose of
chocolate and sugar from Greta's pastry case.

Sam stood, marveling over the sweets Greta had lined
up that day. The café owner was in rare form, pulling out
all the stops on this Thursday afternoon. Sam hadn't had
time to linger earlier when grabbing Yolanda's lemon
bars, but now she noticed the caramel eclairs with pieces
of caramel popcorn on top, raspberry strudels, peach and
passion fruit Danishes, jam Berliners, and sliced pieces of
"Death by Chocolate" cake.

"What's lookin' good today?" Greta said, wiping her
hands on her apron.

"I can't decide if I want chocolate or caramel," Sam
said.

"Life is tough, isn't it?" Greta pulled out one of each
and winked at Sam. "Two for one special today, only for
Pets Reporters."

Sam smiled. She didn't want to go over her argument

with Tom with Greta, but Greta could obviously tell Sam was feeling weighed down and having a tough day.

Sam slid a couple of bucks into Greta's tip jar and asked her to put the sweets on her tab. She turned to walk to her favorite table when Greta called back to her.

Sam approached the pastry display case, and saw no one.

Greta's muffled, disembodied voice called out. "Sam, you didn't grab a croissant, did you?"

Sam spoke to the pastry case. "Um, no, Greta. Still having problems with the croissant thief?"

"I swear there were five a minute ago. Now there are three." Greta reappeared behind the case as she stood up. She put her fingers to her chin, thinking. "I just don't get it. It's happening right under my nose." She looked up and surveyed the clientele.

The café was relatively quiet in the afternoon. The mothers' group had gone, and most of the early-morning regulars were at work. Even Mason Reed wasn't in his usual seat, though an empty plate full of crumbs told Sam he had recently left, and eaten a raspberry strudel. There was a couple, a man and woman, who appeared to be tourists—the visors gave them away—sitting in a booth, sharing a waffle heaped with ice cream.

Davis Yates, the dog park blogger, was hunched over his laptop with a latte in front of him. Felicity Long and Olaf were in another booth. Sam walked to her seat and sat down, and Pumpernickel jumped into the seat opposite her.

"Well, that's bold," Sam said. "But no chocolate for

dogs." Pumpernickel whined and leapt down once more, lying under the table.

Sam pulled out her notebook. Thoughts of her and Tom's argument, and things she should have said, and shouldn't have, flooded her mind. She tried to push them away to concentrate.

Who were her suspects? She had ruled out Summer Salander and the controversial document, which had just been Henrietta's personal vendetta against dog exercise classes. There was Dana Tripp, who was now inheriting the sanctuary, though she seemed overwhelmed by running it herself. She had been cagey about where she had been the afternoon of the murder. Maybe she was just a good actress.

Then there was the pacifier that Sam had found at Henrietta's. Julie had said it was hers, but Sam had seen Clara with the same pacifier with her son. And Julie, with her wavy, dark hair, could be a match for the younger woman Harold had been seen with around town.

Sam thought of Harold next, moving her pencil down her list. Of course, Harold was an obvious choice, but did that make him the wrong one? Occam's Razor stated that the simplest explanation was often the right one. If they weren't legally divorced, then Harold would have gotten Henrietta's rescue and home when she died, but her will had recently been changed to give everything to Dana. And who would want the rescue, which was clearly a money pit, took a whole lot of time to manage, and wasn't turning a profit, or even breaking even?

But then there was the question of the champion

racers. Sam hadn't read anything about that in the previous news stories about Henrietta. Who would know about the dogs? Whoever knew that Henrietta had access to dogs worth thousands of dollars to a breeder might have been willing to kill to get them. That was where it didn't make sense for Clara to kill Henrietta over a gambling grudge with her husband. Sam wished she could rule Clara out. Clara had been so sweet at the barbecue, and Sam really did want to be friends with her. Of course, the most ruthless killers could also be the most charming.

Sam wished she had more details about the golf club, and they would have been easiest to get from Tom. But they hadn't even gotten that far, things had escalated so quickly in the newsroom.

Sam walked over to grab a *Bugle* copy from Greta's newsstand and returned to her seat. Henrietta's murder was on the front page.

The Monday death of a local dog rescuer has been ruled a homicide, police said.

Police were alerted to a bloody golf club Friday morning, which was found in the front yard of a house in the 4800 block of River Road.

Police have officially identified no suspects, though Clara and Cliff Wilson, occupants of the residence, were both seen being brought in for questioning Friday.

The victim, Henrietta Duveaux, 65, was found dead in her backyard Monday evening, and the golf club is suspected to be the murder weapon. DNA tests will take up to five weeks to return results on the identity of the blood, police said.

Anyone with tips or information can call 555-1010.

Sam studied the images in the paper. There was a crime scene photo of police pulling the golf club out of the ground. There was the profile photo of Henrietta, stone-faced, that she recognized as a cut-out from a photo from the morgue that she and James had found. James! Sam dug through her bag and pulled out the white, unmarked envelope he had left on her desk. Had that been another reason Tom was angry with Sam? Was Tom also annoyed by Sam's budding friendship with James?

Sam ripped open the top and pulled out a photo and a piece of paper with writing on it. The writing read, *"Heard you were working on a difficult assignment. Not sure if this helps? James."*

What difficult assignment? Sam looked at the image, and realized it was a zoomed-in shot of the golf club being carried by one of the police officers on the scene. Why would James have given her this? Then Sam saw it: There were three initials engraved in the side of the golf club: *HSW*.

Sam pulled out the stash of notes she had from the day the greyhounds had escaped. She riffled through them until she came to the interview notes from Clara Wilson's husband. She scanned them and then found it. The reporter had written:

Cliff Joshua Wilson

Sam couldn't remember Harold's middle name. Tom

had all the clippings about his violent past. But that golf club had to be his. It certainly wasn't Cliff's.

Sam's palms grew sweaty. James hadn't been mad at her for digging into the murder like Tom had been. He'd helped her out. Surely this was a detail the police were looking into, but one that hadn't been released to the public. Did Tom know? It was unlikely, if James hadn't showed him the photo.

As she thought back on visiting the morgue with James, Mayor Winston Georges popped into Sam's head again. Then she remembered the young woman identified as his breeder in the next photo spread. It was the same toothy smile she had seen in the photograph at Henrietta's. Priscilla Clavell. Of course. The dog breeding family. Clayton Clavell's mother. Her hobby.

If anyone would know about Henrietta's greyhounds' pedigrees, it would be Priscilla Clavell. If she'd known Henrietta for that many years, she'd be able to tell Sam about Harold, too.

Sam pulled out Clayton's business card and looked at the numbers scrawled on it. She took a deep breath, and dialed the one for the direct line.

"Hello?" said a woman's voice.

"Oh, um, Clayton?" Sam said, surprised.

"No, this is Miss Maple. May I ask who is calling?"

"Have I reached Clavell Enterprises?" Sam said, rereading the business card she held in her hand.

"You have reached the Clavell household, ma'am."

Sam petted Pumpernickel under the table with her feet, and the dog snored lightly. "Perfect. In that case, may I speak to Priscilla?"

"I still don't know who is calling," Miss Maple said.

"This is Samantha Hodges. I'm the Pets Reporter for the *Birchwood Bugle*. Her son thought I might be able to do a story on her dog breeding." Sam waited. There was silence on the other end of the line. "Miss Maple?" she asked.

There were two muffled voices from the other end of the phone, and what sounded like arguing.

Then a woman's voice picked up, and it sounded much older than Miss Maple.

"Samantha Hodges," the voice said, drawing out each syllable slowly and richly.

"Miss Clavell?" Sam asked.

"I've been meaning to call you. Clayton mentioned running into your dog at a garden party, and I was just delighted to hear you'd be interested in speaking with me. I think we have a lot to talk about."

"I think we do, too," Sam said. There was something strange in her voice, a note Sam couldn't identify, but knew she'd heard before.

"How about afternoon tea? I would hate to be disrupting a busy day on your news desk."

Busy day. Right, Sam thought. She needed to get Frank her Dog Zumba story, but she figured she could knock it out in an hour. Working on deadlines imposed by editors or breaking news had always motivated her to work quickly, but working on a deadline to solve a murder before the killer got away was even more motivating.

"Wonderful. I'll see you at four?" Sam asked.

"Do you know where we live, dear?" Priscilla said,

and Sam suddenly recognized the feeling. It was when she had spoken to public relations professionals in Chicago. They held a perfect veneer of chipperness, but their motivations were always ulterior. Sam felt uneasy about visiting Priscilla's, but knew that the breeder was her next best lead for finding out more about Henrietta's murder.

"At the top of Ranchwood Hill, yes?" Sam said, furiously Googling the public information on the Clavell family. Her eyes grew wide as she recognized the mansion they lived in. You could see it perched on top of the town's only hill from many vantage points around Birchwood, and Sam and her friends had made up stories in grade school about the eccentric rich people who lived inside. The house bore down on the town, showing off its wealth.

"That's right, Samantha. I'll be waiting for you."

Sam hung up the phone and knew the bike ride up the hill would have pushed her to her limit any other day. But on the day she had also done an hour of Dog Zumba cardio, lifting and bending and stretching and twirling? It would be a doozy.

Sam left the last bites of her chocolate cake and caramel éclair. Strenuous physical activity on a stomach full of sugar would also be a bit difficult, but at least she had a couple of hours to digest.

Greta slipped into the seat opposite Sam. Her rich, dark brown hair was pulled up in a messy bun, and Greta's face had a spot of flour on each side.

"Sam," she said. "There's another croissant missing. I think I'm losing my mind."

"Maybe ask Olaf," Sam said, nodding her head in direction of the giant St. Bernard.

Greta laughed. "A likely culprit. Listen, my tenant is moving out even earlier than expected. You want in?"

Sam's eyes grew wide. "Really? I would love to!" Her acceptance was immediate, but then Sam knew she had to backtrack. "Actually, um, I'm on a bit of rocky terrain at work. I don't know if I'll be the Pets Reporter much longer."

"Geez, Sam, what have you done now?" Greta said, but it wasn't harsh. It was teasing.

"I've been kind of trying to solve Henrietta's murder," Sam said.

"I saw that in the paper today. It's crazy. Well, are you going to do it?" Greta ate the last bites of Sam's desserts.

"Solve it?" Sam fiddled with her pen.

"Sam, the police just found a bloody golf club, and they have no official suspects. I bet you've got more than that."

Greta stood and patted Sam on the back. She lowered her voice, so the other patrons wouldn't hear, which was rare for Greta. "Listen, Sam. So what if you aren't allowed to write about Pets here? Do what you know is right." And with that, Greta was off.

Sam looked at her notebook with the list of names, and then at her laptop screen showing the large Clavell mansion.

CHAPTER EIGHTEEN

She was right: the ride was difficult. It had been fine all the way down Grand Canine Way, the turn onto River Road, then the turn onto Animalia Avenue. But as soon as she set out on the winding, inclined road that led to the top of the hill that held the Clavell mansion, her legs began to scream. Even Pumpernickel panted in the afternoon sun.

Sam's phone rang and she pulled it out with one hand while keeping her other on her handlebars. She didn't recognize the number.

"Hello?" she said.

"Hello, Ms. Hodges. It's Herman, of Herman's Collectibles and Oddities. I have done some amateur detective work and I think you'll be pleased with the results."

Sam's bike wobbled. If she had been zooming down a flat road, holding the phone in one hand would have been no problem. But it was the steep incline, and her slow pace, that made her fumble with her bicycle. Pumpernickel looked up and gave Sam a wide berth.

"Yes, Herman? I'm listening."

"I think you'll be really pleased."

Sam remembered Herman's shy eagerness to be included in the investigation, and could tell he wanted an honorary sheriff's badge. Or at least a gold star.

"Herman, I'm really impressed that you've found something, but I didn't doubt for a second you would. I'd been waiting for your call." Was she laying it on too thick?

Sam could practically hear Herman smiling over the phone. Nope, just right.

"Well, I realized I had a ticket I hadn't entered into my logbook. It fell under the counter." Herman's voice became a bit sheepish.

"But now you've found it! What did it say?" Sam tried to be perky. She also tried not to breathe loudly, as she felt her heart thumping and a line of sweat dripped down the side of her face, not, however, because she was excited about Herman's revelation; in fact, she suspected it might not be a big piece of information.

"Around 5:00 p.m. on Monday, some of those heirlooms came into the shop," Herman said.

Sam stopped pedaling in a moment of surprise, but on the inclined hill, it wasn't such a good idea. As her bicycle stopped and then began to move backward, Sam began pedaling again. Six p.m. was the time of Henrietta's murder. So whoever pawned the items had plenty of time to return to the Retired Racer Rescue and kill

Henrietta. She checked her watch, and it was 3:45 p.m. She didn't have time to stop. She started pedaling again.

"Who—" she breathed in sharply. "Who was it, Herman?"

"My ticket says Dana Trap, home address on Oak Boulevard," Herman said.

"Dana Tripp?" Sam asked.

"Oh, yes, I'm sorry, that's it!" So that's where Dana had been when she'd said she had taken the day off early because she was sick. But why had she lied about it? Had Henrietta asked Dana to pawn those items? Not likely, otherwise, wouldn't Dana have mentioned it?

"Great, thank you, Herman. And have any more pieces from that set come in?"

"I've been watching this place like a hawk," Herman said, his voice serious. "I'm sorry I wasn't sweeping under the counter like one, though."

"Don't worry, Herman, you've really helped me with a breakthrough in my investigation. But I'm sorry, I've got to go," Sam pressed the red "end call" button on her phone before Herman could protest.

So Dana was stealing from her employer. It wouldn't have been a stretch of the imagination that she wanted to steal and sell the prized racing champions at top dollar, then. Was she in cahoots with Harold West? After all, the golf club evidence pointed to him. Maybe the two, who had both disliked Henrietta for their own reasons, had decided to do her in and profit. Sam would just clinch the final piece of the puzzle when she spoke to Priscilla Clavell. If Priscilla could confirm that Harold and Dana had both known about the champion racers, then it would all fall into place.

Harold had been supposed to inherit the rescue when Henrietta died, and he would have gotten access to those prized greyhounds worth thousands. But he hadn't actually wanted the rescue, so he'd gotten in cahoots with Dana, and they'd convinced Henrietta to leave the rescue to Dana. Now Harold could marry his new, young lover, and not have to worry about Henrietta's interference or refusal to grant him a divorce.

Sam's thoughts raced. The young woman had probably gone to ask for Henrietta's approval of her and Harold's relationship that afternoon, hence the dropped pacifier, and when Henrietta had denied it, Harold and Dana had moved forward with their plan. Maybe Priscilla Clavell had even bought dogs from the Retired Racer Rescue, and had the receipts to prove just how much the dogs were worth. As much as she disliked the man, Sam would tell Dan Jasper what she knew, and the case would be resolved.

Sam wouldn't need to take it any further. She'd have all the time in the world to devote to her new job, move into Hygge House, and patch things up with Tom. Sam suddenly felt a sharp pang of regret in her stomach. Tom. She wished she hadn't been so quick to anger with him earlier. He was one of her oldest friends. Reacting sharply in high-stress situations was a weakness of hers, she had to admit. After all, wasn't her very poor reaction —if an unconscious and uncontrollable one, at that—at that press conference what had driven her out of Chicago and into this mess in the first place?

Well, it ended tonight. She'd gather what she could from Priscilla, bike home, and call Dan Jasper. Hopefully he'd handle the investigation well, which Sam doubted a bit.

A police siren whoop from directly behind her made Sam jump and seize her handlebars, though this time she managed to steady them, as she hadn't been able to in front of Cathy Stilkington's blue Honda sedan, or when Pumpernickel surprised her.

She kept pedaling, and a police cruiser pulled up next to her.

"I'm trying to pull you over," Detective Jasper shouted. "And now you're evading police."

"Me?" Sam asked. "I'm on a bicycle."

"I know that," Jasper said. "Now pull over!"

Sam pulled her brakes and stopped on her bike. If she'd been in a car, she'd have stayed seated, so she did that now.

"Please get out of the—" he stopped himself. "Er, please exit your vehicle."

Sam put her kickstand up and got off of her bike. Pumpernickel stood off the road in the grass, her tail wagging limply. She whimpered.

"You were driving a vehicle while talking on a cell phone, a serious infraction," Jasper said.

"It's a bicycle!" Sam said.

"As I am aware. But it is a vehicle, and you are endangering lives."

"But—"

"If you resist, I can also tack on your failure to pull over during a police siren."

Sam shut her mouth as Jasper wrote down on his notepad. "What's your name again, reporter?" Sam had half a mind to give him a fake name, but didn't.

"Sam Hodges," she said.

He tore the paper off of his notepad and handed Sam a $75 ticket.

"Now, in the back of the cruiser," Jasper said.

"Wait, am I being arrested, too? You can't arrest me for a non-arrestable offense."

Jasper looked her in the eyes with his piercing, icy stare, and Sam guessed he hadn't banked on her knowing a bit about the law. His intimidation probably worked on some, but it wouldn't work on a former crime reporter.

He tried to smile, but it looked forced, and gave his face the effect of being even more menacing than when he had actually been staring menacingly.

"I'm visiting the Clavell residence. As you're on this road, I'm guessing that's your destination as well. Would you like a ride?"

"A ride?" Sam said, taken aback.

Pumpernickel raced forward, panting, and eyed the cruiser. She hopped on her feet, though Sam wondered if it was the hot pavement and not excitement.

If Sam had been alone, no matter how sweaty or hot or exhausted she was, she would have made that bicycle ride instead of relying on Jasper for support. She inherently didn't trust him. But she had Pumpernickel now, and had to think of the skinny dog. Sam had foolishly forgotten to bring water, and she could see Jasper had several bottles in the cup holders of his cruiser.

He saw where she was looking.

"Hot out here, huh?" His grin widened.

"And my bike?" Sam asked.

"It will fit in the trunk," he said.

"Okay, but I'm not sitting in the back." Sam nodded toward the cage where criminals were put behind wire fencing.

"Either you or the dog have to," Jasper said.

Three minutes later, the cruiser was slowly rolling up the single road that led to the Clavell mansion. Sam and Pumpernickel were both in the back, with Sam holding a plastic Tupperware container that she guessed had once held Detective Jasper's lunch. Now it held fresh, cool water that Pumpernickel eagerly lapped. Sam declined to drink any. As the trees rushed past, she wondered why Jasper was heading to the Clavells' too. Maybe he had worked out what she had. But she doubted it. Well, if she could talk with Priscilla, she wouldn't even have to wait to call Jasper. He could find out right there and then. Maybe it was good luck, the residual effect of Greta's strawberry lemon bars.

Jasper pulled the squad car up in front of the Clavell mansion and turned the ignition off. The house was huge, and surrounded by an even bigger lawn with bright green grass. A few hedges were shaped into dogs, and a three-car garage was attached to the large, limestone brick home. The front archway was massive, and Sam could see a chandelier hanging in the high entryway. Off to the side, a gaggle of Golden Retrievers romped in a fenced-in area, and jumped into a dog-bone shaped swimming pool. Behind their area, Sam saw what looked like a larger swimming pool for humans.

Sam slid along the seat towards the door, and had a quick thought that Jasper could leave her and Pumpernickel inside the car when he went inside, as the doors couldn't be opened from the inside.

But he walked to the back and unlatched one. "C'mon, reporter," he said. "Let's get this over with."

CHAPTER NINETEEN

Jasper rang the bell, and he, Sam, and Pumpernickel waited on the large stone porch. The entryway to the home was even larger than it had appeared from the car, and Sam felt dwarfed by the massive wooden doors.

One was pulled open, and a young woman with a tight bun of black hair and a conservative black skirt suit smiled at them. "Miss Clavell will see you in the tea room," she said. Sam guessed it was Miss Maple.

Jasper and Sam walked through the door, but Miss Maple gasped.

"Oh! I'm sorry, no dogs allowed in the house." She rushed toward the door, and Sam turned to see Pumpernickel back away, crouching in fear from the woman coming at her, arms outstretched.

"Hey!" Sam said, quickly trotting back two steps and putting herself in between the dog and Miss Maple.

Sam's eyes were still adjusting from the bright sunlight to the dimly-lit entryway. What was the point of all that fancy crystal hanging above her if it didn't really work as an effective lighting source? But she could see a figure practically jumping down the stairs, taking them two at a time.

"I've got it, Georgette," Clayton Clavell said.

He was wearing a similar outfit to the one Sam had seen him in at the barbecue. Different polo shirt, though.

"I'm sorry, um, Samantha, right? I'll just take her to where we keep our dogs. I promise she'll be well looked after."

Pumpernickel looked up at Sam, her eyes wide. Sam knelt down next to her. The two hadn't been apart for long in the four days they'd spent together, and Sam was becoming used to having the retired racer at her side.

She put her hands on Pumpernickel's side, pressing in gently. Sam had seen Frances do that to soothe and calm her own dogs, and the many other dogs she had come in contact with over her career.

"I'll come get you as soon as I'm finished in here," Sam said.

Jasper snorted, but when Sam whipped her head back to glare at him, he began to pretend he was having a coughing fit.

"All right, then," Clayton said, and he affixed a lead to Pump's collar and walked through the door. Miss Maple closed it behind him.

"Right," she said, clasping her hands together. "To the sitting room."

Sam and Jasper walked to the left of the entryway, through another large set of doors, and into a room that had what Sam guessed must be antiques to decorate it.

Sam felt like she was walking onto the set of Downtown Abbey. She wondered how it was that people seemed to have worse taste the more money they had. It looked pristine, like a museum, not a home. She thought longingly of the Hygge House apartment that could be hers, if she wrapped up this investigation and got back to focusing on her Pets Reporter job. It was almost over.

Miss Maple instructed them to sit, and Jasper and Sam chose opposite ends of a long couch. Jasper sat up straight and took off his hat, twirling it in his hands. Sam rolled her eyes at his nervous tic. She tried to remain still, but was uncertain what Priscilla would say, and if she would say it in front of Jasper.

It was a few minutes later that a woman who must be Priscilla opened another door, not the one that Sam and Jasper had entered through. She smiled, but her lips were pursed tightly, so Sam couldn't notice much resemblance with the old photos she'd seen of Priscilla in the *Bugle* archives and at Henrietta's. She remembered that James, as a super-recognizer, would have been able to spot her instantly, smile or not. She realized she had the clue of the golf club, the photo, in her bag. But she didn't want to hand it over. Not yet. And Jasper had the golf club, so certainly he already knew about the initials carved on it.

Miss Maple entered the room next, carrying a tray of tea and finger sandwiches. The tea pot and cups must be fine china. Sam wondered how much they'd fetch at Herman's.

"Coffee, anyone?" Priscilla said. "So silly of me, I only drink tea, but I figure you do such hard work on the police force, it must be tiring."

Hard work like being outrun in a police chase by cyclists going uphill, Sam thought. She was already eating a finger sandwich. Sam ached for water, and wished she had accepted some in the police cruiser. Her silly reactions again, she thought. At least she was taking better note of them.

"Oh no, Mrs. Clavell, trying to cut back," Jasper said. He winked as he picked up the teacup. "Some tea will do me good, I think."

Sam could tell he was putting on an extra bit of flair for Sam's sake, showing off that Priscilla was doting on him but not the pesky reporter.

Priscilla smiled. "I find lemon-rose very good for vitality and clear-thinking."

Sam would have loved a cup of coffee over tea, but it seemed Priscilla's offer had not been directed at her, despite her mention of "anyone."

All the exercise she had done that day had left her starving. She grabbed another finger sandwich, and extended a teacup for Miss Maple to pour some lemon-rose in. Sam needed clear thinking. She had to solve this case, with Jasper watching. Maybe she'd be able to make him think he'd figured it out. In any case, her linguistic gymnastics would have to be on point in this stuffy room. She heard a dog bark and looked out the window, seeing two Golden Retrievers wrestling, but no sign of Pumpernickel. Where had Clayton taken her?

"Now, Mrs. Clavell, let's please go over what you wanted to discuss," Jasper said, taking the lead of the discussion while Sam had her mouth full. Sam was still trying to figure out how to go about this interview, but decided she'd sit back and watch for a bit to see what Jasper's game was.

"Well." Priscilla cleared her throat. "I just want to say before we begin, that it is such a tragedy that Henrietta Duveaux was murdered in cold blood. May she rest in peace," Priscilla said, looking at Sam.

"It is one of the saddest cases I've seen in my career," Jasper said, looking down at his teacup in his hands.

Sam tried not to let her mouth fall open. First of all, because it was full of mayonnaise and cucumber finger sandwiches (a disgrace Greta would have nearly died over), but also because she couldn't believe the posturing going on at the other side of the couch. Jasper was laying it on thick.

The three of them sat in silence. Sam chewed slowly.

"You had a relationship with Henrietta, is that right?" Jasper asked.

"Yes, I knew Henrietta in school as young girls. We fell out of touch when I moved to New York, but when I returned to Birchwood to marry Richard Clavell, Henrietta had already started her dog rescue. We had similar interests, Damon."

Jasper nearly choked on a bit of finger sandwich, and Sam glanced at him. So Priscilla wasn't his good friend. She didn't even know his name was Dan. Sam felt emboldened.

"Similar interests like greyhounds with champion pedigrees?" Sam said.

"You were buying champion racers from Henrietta," Jasper said quickly, and Sam knew he was trying to regain ground in front of her. So he did know.

"It was a secret that we bought champion racers off of Mrs. Duveaux," Priscilla began. "Henrietta had a good relationship with the owners of the racetrack, but she wanted to keep it that way, and news spreading about her income from the dogs would certainly raise eyebrows about what sort of rescue she was really running." Priscilla took a long sip of tea and replaced the cup in the saucer she was holding with a clink.

She smoothed her floral, cream-colored dress over her knees, and sat on the edge of an antique chair. Sam and Jasper waited. She sighed.

"Henrietta needed the money, and we were glad to support the rescue."

"But Harold wasn't happy about it?" Sam said. She couldn't stop herself. She needed to know, and was eager to get to the resolution of this whole saga.

"Harold knew about the value of some of the dogs, yes," Priscilla said. "I believe Miss Tripp also became aware but did not approve of the practice. She thought Henrietta should have been doing more promotion in town, not discreetly selling a few high-priced dogs to raise money."

Well, Sam thought, *there you go. Dana did it. What else did Henrietta have that someone would want, besides a few cheap European heirlooms that were a dime a dozen in pawnshops across suburban America?*

"From the reporter's interest," Priscilla said, referring to Sam, "I gather that she now knows as well."

Jasper and Priscilla kept their eyes locked on each other, as though Sam wasn't there also, listening to the conversation about her.

Priscilla continued, "If a reporter knows, I can't imagine how many other people she's told. I guess it is now an open secret, as many in this town have nothing better to do with their time than gossip. If everyone in town knew that dog was worth a fortune, I imagine anyone could have gone after Henrietta to acquire it. In fact, someone might have done so to stop us from acquiring it."

"I didn't tell anyone," Sam said. Priscilla and Jasper turned to Sam. "It was someone who already knew. So it had to be—"

Priscilla didn't let her finish.

"If you didn't tell anyone," Priscilla said, her eyes boring into Sam. "Then the only one with motive to steal a dog, I'm afraid, would be you."

"Me?" Sam said. She swallowed. "What would I want with a greyhound?"

"You arrived with one today, did you not?" Priscilla said.

"Pumpernickel?" Sam said, as Jasper stood.

Priscilla continued talking as Jasper moved toward Sam. "It's no secret that you've been unemployed for a while now. How convenient that you found Henrietta murdered when you went there to interview her."

Sam instinctively leaned back as Jasper got closer. "But—"

"Miss Hodges, you're under arrest for the murder of Henrietta Duveaux," Jasper began. "Anything you say can and will be used against you ..."

Sam spoke over him as she realized ... "Pumpernickel is the champion racer?"

"And it doesn't help your case that you're already breeding her," Priscilla said, as Jasper pulled Sam up by the arm and turned her around to clasp the handcuffs on her.

"Breeding her?" Sam said, turning her head back over her shoulder, directing her question at Priscilla. The handcuffs clicked on.

"Yes. Pumpernickel is pregnant."

CHAPTER TWENTY

Sam sat in Jasper's office with a cup of coffee. She was handcuffed by one wrist to the chair, and had one free hand for sipping. It showed how peaceful and small of a town Birchwood was that there wasn't even a cold, gray, concrete interview room with a single lightbulb hanging from the ceiling. Greta would have been disappointed from her years of watching crime shows, Sam thought.

Not that Detective Dan Jasper's office wasn't cold in its own way. He had barely any personal objects around his desk or the shelves behind it. There was a notepad, closed, with two pens on it. A stack of old *Birchwood Bugles* was in a recycling bin on the floor next to the desk. Sam could see Henrietta's photo looking up at her. Sam leaned forward over the desk, noticing there was one lone picture frame near Jasper's phone. She could barely see that the photo was of a younger Jasper with a young woman. Wife? Girlfriend?

Sam leaned back in the chair. Jasper had been gone

for about half an hour, she guessed. Before that, he had pelted her with questions, and she'd tried to convince him that Harold and/or Dana were the true murderers, but he hadn't entertained her theories.

Sam wondered if Greta would show up. Greta had been the only one she could think of to call. Frances would be at work, and her parents, she didn't want to worry. She'd made Greta promise she wouldn't be teasing Sam about this in public, if Sam ever lucked out of this situation.

At least she had had some time to think while Jasper was away. His constant questions certainly didn't allow for it.

It had to be Harold or Dana, but could one have tried to frame the other?

Priscilla had said that Dana didn't like that Henrietta was selling the dogs, that she disagreed about the entire way that Dana was running the rescue. If Sam was working in a place like that which constantly needed money and extra hands, she'd certainly feel personally slighted if her boss wasn't making any effort to raise donations.

Her thoughts drifted to Pumpernickel. Was she okay? It looked like the Clavells treated their dogs like royalty, so they were sure to treat Pumpernickel the same. But certainly, Pumpernickel couldn't be pregnant. Or if she had had a rendezvous at the barbecue or some other time out of Sam's supervision, she wouldn't be showing already, right? Sam had to admit she really knew nothing about animals, and even less about dog gestation periods. How did the Clavells know, anyway? Maybe

Clayton had encouraged the deed himself at the barbecue.

Outside the room, Sam heard voices. It sounded like Jasper and another male voice, one she didn't recognize. They didn't seem aware their voices were carrying into Jasper's office. She heard the name Dana Tripp and her ears perked up.

She picked up the wooden chair with her free hand and her handcuffed one, and wobbled awkwardly a bit closer to the door. Then she stopped, and looked at the desk. She had nothing but her coffee, but it would have to do.

"Sorry," she whispered, as she poured the coffee onto the floor. She then picked up the chair again and began scooting. Setting the chair down by the door, she held the Styrofoam coffee cup to the door and listened.

"A neighbor across from the scene claims they saw a woman with it," the unfamiliar voice said.

With what? Sam thought.

"Are they sure?" Jasper said. "Reliable witness?"

The other voice laughed. "It's not hard to spot one," the other voice said. "Even in a silhouette. The witness was Cathy Stilkington. I play cards with her husband twice a month. Reliable."

Cathy Stilkington! Sam would have fallen off her chair if she hadn't been handcuffed to it. All this time, the person she needed to talk to was the one who'd run her over! But what had she seen?

"Any description of the woman?" Jasper asked.

"Too tall to fit the reporter for sure. Thin. That's about it."

Did that mean Sam was getting off the hook? She wondered where Greta was. Hopefully not letting it slip into the Birchwood rumor mill that Sam had been arrested. Greta was always letting stuff actually slip into the smoothie machine. Birchwood residents with allergies had to avoid them entirely.

"Darn!" Jasper said. "Well, the woman could have been aiding a man, after the fact."

"It's tough to say, sir," the other voice said. "But one thing's for sure. We have to let the reporter go."

Jasper sighed deeply. "Thanks, Johnson."

Sam pulled her head quickly away from the door and threw the coffee cup a few feet in front of her. The door opened about a foot and hit the chair Sam was sitting in.

"What the—" Jasper said.

"Ah, sorry!" Sam said, hopping the chair inch by inch away from the door.

Jasper poked his head through the door and looked at Sam. His face was red with anger.

"What in Lady Justice's name are you doing, reporter?" he almost shouted.

"Trying to clean up," Sam said, pointing to the empty coffee cup and small drips of coffee on the floor. "Sorry, clumsy." She raised her hands, open-palmed, and shrugged her shoulders in the international sign for "I don't know."

Jasper looked as if he didn't believe her, but had no way to prove it.

"Well, you're free to go," Jasper said, squeezing through the doorframe.

"And Pumpernickel?" Sam said. "I want my dog

back." She hadn't expected "my dog" to come out of her mouth.

"It sounds like the dog didn't belong to you," Jasper said. "I'm so sick of these animals!"

"Then you won't last long in Birchwood," Sam said.

Jasper looked at her, and for the first time, Sam saw him as more than a thorn in her side with an attitude problem.

He looked exhausted. "I just can't figure this out," he said. He unlocked Sam's wrist with the key and walked behind his desk, sitting down, and burying his head in his hands.

Sam felt sorry for him. She wanted to help him in some small way, but didn't want to ask any questions that would let on that she had been listening at the door. So she'd at least help him with sorting out the Pumpernickel issue. He certainly wouldn't want the dog becoming his custody as he tried to sort out the legality.

"Listen, call, um ... Dana Tripp ... to ask about Pumpernickel. She'll tell you she asked me to foster the dog. And—" Sam reached into the recycling bin. Jasper looked at her like she was crazy. "Here."

Sam flipped through a two-day old *Birchwood Bugle*, folded it over, and placed it on Jasper's desk. "Here's a story I wrote about asking volunteers to come forward to foster dogs from the rescue. It's not a special situation."

Jasper looked down at the newspaper. "That all should be easy enough." He leaned back in his chair. "And I have to go to the Clavell household again anyway, because I'm pretty sure that Clayton kid is the one who cut a hole in the fence."

"What?" Sam asked. Even though he was at least four years older than Sam, she thought the "kid" reference was apt.

Jasper sighed. "The neighbor, Charlie Hume, saw him." Sam silently kicked herself for not thinking to ask Charlie what else he might have seen at Henrietta's. "It makes sense, after all, that he wanted that dog. But the Clavells donate so much money to the police force here, it's going to be quite an assignment."

Jasper seemed tired at the thought of it. Sam didn't envy his position.

"But you don't think he killed Henrietta?" Sam asked.

"Not him, or the Wilsons, which would have made my job easy. They were both home at the time of the murder, and phone records confirm it," Jasper said. "Hume even saw a woman with a stroller visiting 518 Wichitaw Way the day of the murder, so that would have made it simple if it were Mrs. Wilson."

Sam felt relieved. It officially wasn't Clara, which she already knew, but it was nice to know her new friend wouldn't be harassed by the police anymore. And that meant Sam didn't have to bring up the pacifier.

"But the woman with the stroller," Sam began slowly, waiting for Jasper's reaction. He sat still. "I think she may have been Harold West's young lover."

Jasper laughed. But Sam continued, "Henrietta wouldn't grant Harold a divorce years ago when he wanted to marry a younger woman. Maybe killing her this time was the only way."

"Nice try, reporter," Jasper said, folding his arms

across his chest. "But Harold Sylvester West has been cleared by us since day one. He had an AA meeting the night of the murder. We have about 12 witnesses to his innocence."

"AA?" Sam said. Her head spun. "But what about ..."

Jasper's face hardened, his lips becoming a thin line across his face. Sam knew that she'd gone too far, asking one question too many. Something seemed to trigger Jasper's memory that he was in the presence of a reporter, not a fellow police confidante, just like her questions had the night of Henrietta's murder. Sam wouldn't get any more questions answered, but she didn't mind. She was just glad she wasn't handcuffed to the chair anymore, and facing murder charges.

Jasper straightened up his back and stood. His voice was sharp again. "Okay, come on. Your friend is waiting for you, Hodges."

Jasper walked over and opened the door for Sam.

His curtness and coldness had returned, but he wasn't yelling like when they'd first met. Maybe he held something like respect for her now. After all, he was calling her something besides "reporter" now. Sam tried to stifle her smile.

Ten minutes later, Sam was walking out of the police station doors with Greta by her side. The sun had set on Birchwood, and yellow streetlamps illuminated their walk. When they were safely down the block from the station, walking in the direction of Hygge House down a tree-lined street, the silhouettes falling over the road, Sam and Greta were nearly bursting to talk.

"Okay," Sam said. "How did you get me out of there?"

"I had security camera footage of you in Hygge House basically all day before Henrietta's murder Monday. Would have taken me ages to find old newspapers and figure out the time of the murder, but thankfully Mason Reed was there, so I just asked him, found the right time and date, and basically ran over here with the evidence exonerating you. I had half a mind to prep it sooner, seeing as, with all the poking around you were doing, I thought Jasper would come after you, but well, I left it until the last minute. Sorry, Sam."

Sam was astounded, and impressed by her friend. Maybe it was good that Greta watched so much CSI and Law & Order. "Sorry? Greta, you saved me!"

Great leaned in and gave her friend a hug. She then pulled back and looked Sam in the eye. "I have to show you something else I saw on the security camera footage, too." Looking around, she asked, "Wait, where's Pumpernickel?"

"Over at the Clavells'," Sam grumbled.

"Wait, and your bicycle?" Greta said.

"Ugh," Sam groaned. "Probably in evidence." Sam pictured her bicycle, a crosswalk, a blue Honda sedan, and a man dressed as the Statue of Liberty.

She suddenly stopped walking, and Greta stopped two steps later.

"Are you okay?" Greta asked.

"Greta, where does Cathy Stilkington live?"

"Oh, umm," Greta said. "Over on River Road, I'm pretty sure. Why? Did she steal your bicycle? What's up with that woman?"

Sam looked into the distance, her thoughts swirling. She suddenly knew. If it had been a tall, thin woman carrying that object—something long and thin that you wouldn't mistake, even in silhouette—on River Road, it had to have been the murderer burying the murder weapon.

Everyone had an alibi now except one person.

"Greta, I'm sorry, I have to go," Sam said.

"Wait, what?" Greta called after her, as Sam bounded away toward Oak Boulevard.

Sam wished she had time to go back to the station and remind Jasper to return her bicycle, but who knew how long that would take, how difficult he would make it, how much paperwork there would be.

No, Sam didn't have time, she thought, as she looked at her watch. If it was an hour's drive to O'Hare airport from Birchwood, she had less than half an hour to stop a murderer from fleeing town.

CHAPTER TWENTY-ONE

S am wasn't too late. She saw a light on in the upstairs
condo where Dana Tripp lived. Dana was catching
a flight to Georgia to help her father move into the
nursing home, and Sam doubted Birchwood would see
the likes of her ever again. She'd have gotten away with it.

Sam pressed the buzzer marked "D. Tripp."

No one answered.

Sam hopped from foot to foot, anxious to get up to
the apartment, and not catch Dana on her way down,
where she'd be able to run off easily.

It took what felt like a dozen rings, but then Dana
picked up.

"Yes?" she said, sounding out of breath.

"Dana, it's Sam," Sam said.

"Sam, I'm packing. The trip to visit my father. I'm
running late. I'm sorry, I can't help you now."

"It's important," Sam said, her voice rising an octave.
She couldn't let Dana get away.

"I'm sorry, Sam," Dana said, and Sam knew she was about to be hung up on.

"It's about Pumpernickel," Sam said quickly.

There was silence.

"Dana?"

Silence.

Then, "Come up," and the buzzer sounded.

Sam bounded up the three flights of stairs in Dana's condo complex. The door to her condo was open, and Sam caught sight of a flash of color moving through the room. Dana was racing from her bed to her dresser and back, stuffing clothes in an old leather travel bag. She looked like she hadn't showered yet from a day at the rescue. Her apartment was small, about half the size of the apartment Sam hoped to rent at Hygge House. But Sam couldn't let her thoughts drift to Hygge House—not yet. Not until this was over.

Sam hadn't thought ahead of any plan, and now here she was, she realized, confronting a murderer.

"So," Dana said, glancing up briefly from her packing rush. "Where's Pumpernickel?" Her voice held an accusatory note.

"That's the thing," Sam said. "She's at the Clavells' due to a ... a misunderstanding. And you need to call Detective Jasper to let him know she can come back with me."

Sam regretted it the moment it was out of her mouth.

Dana suddenly stopped moving, stood up straight, and folded her arms.

"I need to call Detective Jasper? That jerk didn't want to hear anything I had to say except for accusing me of murdering my boss!" Dana suddenly seemed to remember what she had been doing and jumped back into packing. "My taxi was supposed to be here 10 minutes ago!" She didn't particularly say it to Sam, but bellowed it in frustration.

Well, in that case, Sam had better come out with it.

"Did you, Dana?"

"Did I what?" Dana asked, pulling out different T-shirts from a drawer of her dresser.

"Did you kill Henrietta?" Sam said softly. Dana stopped moving. "Someone saw you carrying a golf club to Clara Wilson's yard to bury it. Were you hoping to frame her? Or Harold, by using his golf club? Either would have worked, right? As long as you could assume control of a dog rescue you thought wasn't doing things the right way."

Dana turned slowly, and Sam suddenly feared she had pulled a gun from the drawer. But her hands were empty. Her eyes popped wide when she had turned fully, and they looked over Sam's shoulder.

Sam didn't want to fall for it. Dana was trying to get her to turn around.

Sam swallowed, and tried to steady her voice. "Dana, the police are on their way. It's over. It's okay. The dogs will be taken care of. I'll—I'll make sure of it." Sam could feel her palms growing sticky with sweat. She longed for Pumpernickel by her side.

"Why does everyone care so much about those stupid little skinny dogs?" said a cool voice behind Sam. Sam's body was suddenly electrified. She began slowly to turn her head.

"Don't move," the voice said. "Raise your arms. I've got a gun."

A chill ran up Sam's spine. She looked at Dana, who made eye contact with Sam and nodded. Facing each other, the two women slowly raised their arms in unison.

CHAPTER TWENTY-TWO

"Please," Dana said, her voice pleading.

"Shut up!" the voice said. Sam heard footsteps, coming closer. The woman came into Sam's view on her left side, and Sam recognized the woman from the mothers group. It was the dark-haired woman. Harold's lover. Julie. The three women were now feet apart in Dana's small apartment.

"I didn't want to frame Clara," Julie said, turning to Sam, her voice regretful. "That was unfortunate. But you're right. Dana makes much more sense. I should have buried the club in her yard. Of course, it will make the police work very easy when they realize the reporter confronted the killer, got shot, and the killer turned the gun on herself. They can just look at this copy of Henrietta's will, where you showed her to make changes, Dana."

Julie pulled a folded stack of papers out of her pocket and waved them in the air.

"I had no idea Henrietta would change her will," Dana said. "I thought you were still living in New York."

"What was I supposed to do?" Julie shouted, waving the gun around. Sam cringed, afraid it might go off at any second. "She never exactly made me feel welcome here."

"You didn't have to kill her to be with Harold," Sam said.

"What?" Julie spat.

"Marriage is just a piece of paper," Sam said. "You didn't need it to prove your love."

Julie looked at Sam as if she were crazy, which given the circumstances, felt quite unfair to Sam.

"That's disgusting," she said finally. She looked at Dana. "What's wrong with her?"

But as soon as Julie turned her head to look at Dana, she was surprised by Dana coming at her. As Dana lunged, her arms reached out in front of her, toward the gun that Julie held. But Julie, a split second sooner, moved her hand upward, and out of Dana's grasp.

Dana tumbled forward, crashing onto the floor with a bang.

Julie turned to face the entryway of Dana's apartment, so she could keep Sam, and now Dana's heap, on the floor within her sights.

Sam was still trying to work out why Julie hadn't agreed about being with Harold.

Julie continued, "Well, Dana. It's time to pay for what you've done. You helped Henrietta sell off those heirlooms. Thankfully, Clara told me about seeing them in the pawnshop a few weeks ago. I loved those heirlooms. Henrietta was punishing me. After all these years.

I left her alone with her dogs. Even when I came back, I didn't bother her. And then she went and sold those heirlooms, my family heirlooms, for dog kibble." Julie spat the words "dog kibble" as though it was drugs or something of equal illicitness and distaste.

Sam remembered the morgue. James had looked at the picture of the boarding school visit to the rescue, identifying Clara Wilson and Julie in the photo. Sam thought of the similar faces of Julie and Henrietta. Did that mean ...

"You're Henrietta's daughter," Sam said.

"Great work, Sherlock," Julie said.

Sam could feel her heart inside her chest, and there was a dull roaring in her ears. "The pacifier was Jacques'. It wasn't Clara who went to see Henrietta that day, it was you."

Sam thought quickly. So Henrietta had been a cruel boss, and a neglectful mother. If Julie felt so bitter, enough to commit murder, perhaps Sam could appeal to that deep-seated emotional scar.

"Julie," she said. She had heard that you needed to repeat names often in a situation with dangerous people. To remind them of everyone's humanity. "Julie, Jacques needs you. Henrietta wasn't there for you. And that was cruel. You won't be there for Jacques once you have two more murders on your hands, Julie."

"My real name is *Juliette*." She drew out the name in a seamless French accent. "I always hated the anglicized version. And the murders won't be on my hands," she said. "I'm getting away."

A car beeped its horn outside.

"Who's that?" Julie said, her eyes darting from Sam to the window. Julie sidestepped, keeping her gun pointed at Sam, to try to peer outside.

"My ... taxi ..." Dana said. Her eyes were closed, and she was breathing heavily. Sam felt a drip of sweat slowly roll down the side of her face.

Julie's eyes flashed in anger. She stopped moving.

Reporting was Sam's strong suit. Talking down murderers was not. She didn't know what to say next, and so she did what came naturally: she kept Julie talking by asking questions. Sometimes the silence trick worked on sources, but usually, in those cases, those sources weren't pointing guns at their interviewer. Some sources were more difficult, and you had to pry the answers out of them. Well, Sam thought, curiosity killed the cat, but hopefully not the reporter.

"Julie," Sam said. "If you had the argument in the afternoon, why did you come back later? Why with Harold's golf club?"

"Probably because I learned from my parents." Julie smiled wickedly. "I learned from my mother not to let grudges go. That people would only disappoint. I didn't mean to implicate my father by using his golf club. That was an accident. I never think straight when I fly into a rage." She laughed. "Must have gotten that from him, too. We actually repaired our relationship. He's been sober for 15 years, he says. Ever since I graduated boarding school and didn't tell him and Mom and just went to New York. Now he sees me and Jacques once a week. But like father, like daughter. I take after him, and I grabbed that golf club, just like he did when he was an angry drunk, smashing the lamps and putting holes in the wall."

Dana's landline rang. Julie jumped and Sam noticed her hand holding the gun was shaking.

"Who's that?" she said, looking from Sam to Dana, as though they were telepathic.

"Probably the taxi," Sam said.

"Answer it," Julie said, waving the gun from Dana to the phone, which sat on the dresser in-between them. "Tell them you've changed your mind. You don't need a ride. Tell them to go. Then I can take care of this and get out of here."

Dana put her hands over her eyes. She was shaking, and Sam noticed tears streaking down her cheeks. Dana must be in shock, she thought. She had to protect her.

"We're wasting time!" Julie yelled.

"I'll answer it," Sam said. "I'll pretend to be Dana."

"Well, hurry up!" Julie said. Her green eyes were big and wild.

Sam walked sideways to the phone on the dresser like a crab, so she was facing Julie the whole time. Julie followed her movement with the gun.

Sam picked the phone up slowly, and raised it to her cheek as though she were moving in slow motion.

"He—hello?" Sam said.

A familiar voice spoke into her ear.

"Dana Tripp, Detective Dan Jasper. I need to ask you some questions about a dog from the rescue. Peppercorn. No, um, Pumpernickel. Yes, that's it."

Sam made eye contact with Julie, and tried to betray no indication that she wasn't talking to a taxi driver.

"Hello, driver. Thank you for coming, but I won't be needing a ride to the airport after all," Sam said.

Julie looked on. Sam swallowed.

"No, this is Detective Dan Jasper," Detective Jasper said. How could Sam alert him to what was going on, without giving it away to Julie? Sam rolled her eyes, as though annoyed at the person on the other end of the phone, which she kind of was.

Sam remembered Jasper's embarrassment when Priscilla had called him Damon. Would he know that it was Sam on the other end?

"Damon," she said, putting extra emphasis on the name, "I'm sorry you had to come all the way over here to my house on Oak Boulevard. I know it's inconvenient. And you came so fast. ASAP, like it was an emergency. Yes, I understand. Please stop shouting at me." Sam kept talking, pretending the taxi driver was arguing with her.

"Get it over with!" Julie yelled.

Sam covered the receiver with her hand, but only slightly, hoping that Jasper was still on the line and would hear her through the receiver.

"If he gets angry, Julie, he'll come up here and then he'll see you holding us up. It's better that we make sure he goes peacefully."

But Julie stormed over to the phone, grabbed it from Sam's hand, and slammed it down. She was staring into Sam's eyes and Sam could see a fire burning in them.

Just then a scream erupted from the other side of the room. Julie turned to see Dana's tears being licked by a gray schnauzer who had wandered in through the open door. Dana must have been surprised by the sudden warm, wet tongue over her face. But Sam recognized the dog; they were so much easier to recognize than people.

"These animals!" Julie screamed. Sam tried to walk forward but Julie whipped around and pointed the gun at her. "Not so fast, reporter."

A woman's muffled voice called from the stairwell. "Orion?" she called.

"The dog's owner is coming, Juliette," Sam said. "Let's get him out and close the door."

"I'm not touching him. You do it," she said.

Sam walked over to the door, with Julie pressing the muzzle of the gun into her back the whole way. When the tiny schnauzer saw Sam, he reared up on his hind legs. Sam imagined the flower crown on his head.

"Orion," she cooed. His golden eyes met hers. "Orion," she said again, this time commanding, "You need to leave. Olé!" Sam called, and in perfect Dog Zumba form, Orion raced clockwise around Sam, knocking into one of Julie's legs. She tried to regain balance by reaching for Sam's arm, but Sam was already twirling, just like she had with the other dog owners at Zumba. She twisted her hips, flung her arm in the air, and yelled, "Jump!" to Orion, who knocked the gun from Julie's hand.

Sam tackled Julie to the ground, a move she felt might have been more appropriate in Dog Football than Zumba, but whatever worked. Her life was one crash after another lately, but this was the first tumble that she knew for sure was a Perfect 10.

CHAPTER TWENTY-THREE

Sam sat on the front lawn as more police cruisers showed up, wrapped in a blanket, as most people were after a traumatic incident.

"What's going on here?" Doris had asked as she'd arrived at the door of Dana's apartment to see Sam holding Julie's hands behind her back, Dana on the floor in even more hysterics, and Orion dancing spins around the room and barking.

Doris had called the police to find them already on their way, and the older woman had helped Sam subdue Julie until a man arrived, panting and out of breath, at the door.

But it wasn't Jasper.

Jasper arrived three minutes later.

The first one to arrive was Tom Albers.

"Tom?" Sam said.

"Sam! Are you okay?" He raced into the room. "I'll call—"

"They're on their way," Doris said. "We're quite capable, young man."

Julie writhed under them. "Let me go!" she shouted. "I'll deny everything!"

Sam's own heart was still racing a mile a minute. "You could help Dana," Sam said, nodding in the direction of the woman still lying on the floor.

"Slow your breathing, Dana," Doris called. Tom helped Dana into a sitting position. "Forty years as a nurse," she explained to Sam.

Then Jasper was in the doorway, gun drawn, followed by five more policemen.

Outside, with Julie in the back of a squad car, Jasper interrogated Sam. If she had hoped he'd be more sympathetic after she solved a murder for him, she was wrong.

"Juliette Duveaux admitted the murder to you?" Sam was standing next to the ambulance, and Jasper leaned against it, his strong arm at her face level.

"Yes," Sam said. "Dana will tell you the same thing."

"Motive?" Jasper asked.

"Unfortunately, a lifetime of neglect," Sam said, shaking her head sadly. "But most recently, the selling of priceless French family heirlooms sparked her matricide."

"We'll see what we can get out of her at the station," he said. "And we have to wait until tomorrow to get a statement from Dana; she's too shaken up now. Won't respond to any questions or even look or talk to us."

"And are you getting me Pumpernickel?" Sam asked.

"You're thinking about a dog at a time like this?" Jasper asked. "This town!" he groaned.

But a familiar bark rang through the street. Neighbors had come out of their homes to gawk at what was going on at the four-story condo building, and Sam knew almost no one in town would need to wait to read the paper tomorrow to know what happened. The rumor mill would start churning. A brindle streak raced toward Sam, and Sam knelt and pulled the dog close to her chest.

She buried her face in the dog's neck, and Pumpernickel wiggled with the strong shake of her tail.

"I knew you'd want to see that dog as soon as possible," Greta's voice said, and Sam looked up to see the baker coming toward her.

"How did you—"

"As soon as you raced away, I just knew you were getting yourself into trouble, but it was useless to try to stop you. I called Tom, figuring he would know what mumbo jumbo you were talking about, and when I told him when you'd asked about River Road, he knew you were coming to Dana's. He was out at the zoo at an interview about vandalism on the elephant exhibit, so the drive back was a bit long,"

"I otherwise never drive over the speed limit," Tom said, as he approached. Jasper had disappeared. Tom was smiling sheepishly, and Sam knew their earlier argument was still on his mind. She felt it didn't matter much; just having had her life almost come to an end, she just appreciated that he was there.

"I said I would head to get Pumpernickel from the

Clavells. Might as well take care of a few things for my best friend while I had Mason Reed watching the café."

"Mason Reed?" Sam nearly choked.

"Yeah, my next project is hiring real help, I think," Greta said. "I love that café, but getting away for a bit this afternoon opened my eyes to how good taking some time off can be. And then I can be your Watson, solving murders with you!"

Sam snorted. "Right, Greta. I'm pretty sure this is a once-in-a-lifetime event for Birchwood." She straightened, keeping one hand on Pumpernickel's head. "Greta, Tom, I can't thank you guys enough. You came through when I needed you. But I need to help someone else." She looked down at Pumpernickel.

"C'mon, Pump. There's someone you need to see"

Sam walked Pumpernickel to where Dana sat in the back of an ambulance, a faraway look in her eyes.

"Dana," Sam said, "Pumpernickel wanted to see you."

Pumpernickel jumped up and put her front paws across Dana's lap, sniffing up at her face and wagging her tail furiously. Dana looked down at the dog and her lips curled into the faintest smile. "Pumpernickel," she whispered.

This excited Pump, who then spun in three circles before hopping from foot to foot. She barked in triumph, and Dana laughed.

"Dana," Sam said. "Have you missed your flight?"

"My father!" Dana said, suddenly coming back to reality enough to realize.

"Why don't you give me his number?" Sam said. "I'll

call and let him know you'll be on a flight first thing tomorrow morning. If you give Jasper a statement, he'll let you leave town. You can keep Pumpernickel overnight for company."

"Thank you, Sam," Dana said, letting out a long sigh. "It's been a rough night."

"I understand," Sam said. "But I'm sure you know how good of a companion Pumpernickel is. She's been by my side through a lot the last four days."

Dana smiled and nodded, and Sam could see the tear that ran out of her eye was one of relief and gratitude, not sadness or shock this time.

"I realized I had successfully fostered out all the greyhounds before my trip to Georgia, and couldn't even get a comfort dog tonight if I wanted," Dana said. "It's been the longest two days without any dogs at the sanctuary. I can call my father and rebook my flight. Thank you, Sam. I feel more me with the dog here."

"I get it," Sam said. She patted Pumpernickel.

"Dana," Sam began, feeling a bit hesitant, but not able to resist asking the question. "Why did you sell the heirlooms?"

Dana sighed heavily. "Henrietta had been asking me to sell the heirlooms, yes, but the day she was murdered, I wasn't there on her behalf. The home I'm moving my father into wanted a payment in advance, and it's just so expensive. I figured I would pay her back when I could, but I needed the money upfront. I feel terrible about it."

Sam put her hand on Dana's shoulder. "Well, the rescue is yours now, so now they're all your heirlooms." Sam thought of offering the consolation that Henrietta would have forgiven her, but thought better of it. It didn't sound like the old woman would have.

"I'll give them to Jean-Jacques," Dana said. "They're not worth that much anyway, and there are plenty of ways for the rescue to make money through outreach." She smiled weakly up at Sam. "Especially if we can get coverage occasionally in the *Bugle*."

Sam smiled at Dana, and let her hand fall from her shoulder. "Sure thing, Dana."

Sam walked from the ambulance, and returned to Tom and Greta.

"Well, we better get going," Sam said, readjusting the strap of her messenger bag. "We've got a long night, Tom."

"At the police station?" Greta asked.

"At the newsroom," Sam smiled. "After all, we're just a couple of pesky journalists, not detectives." She pulled out her notebook and pen.

CHAPTER TWENTY-FOUR

It felt like years since the night of Juliette's apprehension, though it had only been two days. Sam had slept most of the day after, waiting at her parents' place to receive Pumpernickel as Dana was on her way to the airport.

That night, miraculously, both Tom and Sam had kept their jobs, even if Tom's article on the graffiti at the zoo had missed deadline, and Sam had nearly gotten herself thrown in jail for murder, and nearly been killed, but she had nevertheless met all her deadlines.

Tom and Sam worked furiously into the night, until the print deadline at 11:30 p.m. Their conversations were professional, and they enjoyed recounting the story to inquiring coworkers when the whole newsroom stopped working for 12 minutes to devour the pizzas that were delivered.

Frank yelled at how stupid the two of them were in his office for a while, but at the end of the night, looking at the front-page proof, "Murderer apprehended by Pets

Reporter and pet," he was smiling, however subtly. Tom and Sam knew that Frank loved a good story more than anything else, and after all, that was what they had gotten him.

Now, Saturday morning, Sam walked into Hygge House, and she could tell from the looks of the patrons that the town was still abuzz 36 hours later about the crazy story of murder in Birchwood.

Greta rushed from behind the counter and grabbed Sam by the arm. "Okay, Pets star. I've got something serious to show you. You, too, Pumpernickel," she said, as the dog slunk behind them. She pulled Sam around behind the counter and pulled up a grainy black and white video on her computer monitor.

"Okay," Greta said. "I may not be the most tech-savvy person in the world, but I'm pretty much a genius for figuring this out."

"Figuring what out? Greta, get on with it. I already know you're a genius; you don't need to convince me," Sam grabbed a fresh caramel roll from where they sat, warming behind the counter, and took a bite. Anyone who could bake like Greta was certainly a genius.

The still image on the computer showed Hygge House, and was clearly from Greta's security camera. Sam figured this was the same camera that had captured her at Hygge House and gotten her out of jail after being suspected of Henrietta's murder.

"Okay, watch this," Greta said, and, while holding the control key on her keyboard, pressed the minus key at the same time. The image zoomed out, and showed more of Hygge House. Greta looked from Sam, back to the computer, and pressed the keys again. The image zoomed out more.

"Greta ..." Sam said.

But Greta pressed play, and pointed to the corner of the screen. As the camera was mounted at the back corner of Hygge House, pointing toward the street, it showed all the seating, the door, and of course, the cash register. But as the camera was just above the pastry case, it only showed a small corner of it.

"I didn't know I was zoomed in," Greta said. "If I zoom out, I can just see the row where I usually put the croissants."

Sam finally got it. "Ah! You caught the pastry thief?"

Greta nodded, and smiled, raising her eyebrows.

"What, Greta? Don't look at me like that!"

The grainy footage jumped to life. A small something was moving into the frame. Like a children's toy ... maybe a rocket? Something long, with a black mark on the end. But then the rocket split into two, opening like a crocodile's mouth. Wait. It was a mouth. A dog's snout. A very thin and long dog snout.

Sam whipped around and saw Pumpernickel sitting stoically, looking at something very interesting on her feet.

Greta pointed to a table by the window, Sam's favorite, in the security camera footage. There sat Sam, buried in her laptop. There was no Pumpernickel near her.

Sam bent down and felt Pumpernickel's stomach now. Pumpernickel rolled over onto her back, expecting a belly rub. Pump's stomach was a bit larger than she remembered it being a week ago, but she hadn't noticed, even after spending so much time with the dog.

"Oh my gosh, she's not pregnant!" Sam said, slapping her forehead. "She's full of carbs!"

"Sam," Greta said sharply, "Don't be rude."

Pump's eyes rose to the two, but her head was still facing downward. The effect was a classic guilty dog look.

"No, no, the Clavells thought Pumpernickel was pregnant!" Sam said. She was relieved to hear that Clayton had been wrong. "Well, thankfully, I've got a one-month pass to the gym, so I think Pump and I are going to be practicing a lot of Dog Zumba to burn off that belly fat."

Pumpernickel's tail began to wag slowly, and she stood up.

"Breakfast is on me," Greta said. "And an appropriate, low-carb doggie treat."

Pumpernickel whined.

Sam made her way to her front table, and a ukulele song began chirping. She picked up her phone.

"Hey, Tom," she said.

"Hey, Sam," he said. "Listen, I—"

"Don't even, Tom," she said. "You don't have to apologize if you just let me move back to the crime desk from Features, where I can tell what day of the week it is by what color cardigan Yolanda is wearing."

"Deal," Tom laughed. "I'll save you a seat on Monday."

"Great," Sam said, smiling a bit sheepishly. She

hadn't realized how much she had missed talking to Tom, even though it had only been two days.

"Great. Look, I've got to go, because I'm meeting Frank in a few minutes to talk about the direction crime is taking at the *Bugle*."

"Wow, that's fantastic," Sam said, "Wait. Does that mean you're the new crime editor?"

"You're looking at him!" Tom said proudly, "Or, er, talking to him, I mean."

"Congrats, Tom," Sam said. "See you soon."

Greta delivered a waffle stacked with bananas, whipped cream, and walnuts to Sam's table.

"A little sweet treat," she said. "And an organic peanut butter dog cookie for this one. Low fat, of course." She laid the treat down in front of Pumpernickel, who gobbled it up in one bite.

"But, let me get out of your way," she said, winking at Sam and looking towards the door. Sam followed Greta's gaze and saw James had just walked through the door, his head hitting the bell overhead it. He had his camera around his neck, and was looking around the café. When he spotted Sam, he smiled and began walking over. He knocked into a chair on the way and apologized to Dachshund Dad and his family.

"Hey, James," Sam said.

"Hi, Sam," he said. "I was taking photos at the dog clothing store and saw you in the window and wanted to say, um, hi, and, congratulations."

Sam blushed. She hadn't been in Birchwood long, but she knew Danielle's Every Day Dog Wear didn't open until 10:00 a.m. most days. And why was James working on a Saturday? Maybe Danielle had opened just for the photoshoot, or maybe ...

"I had another question to ask you, too," James said, and Sam realized it was awkward with him standing and the empty seat next to him.

"Sit," she said. "Help me with this breakfast."

James sat and looked at the mountain of sugar before Sam.

"Is this what you eat for breakfast?"

Sam laughed. "Sometimes. Hey, James, thank you for the printout with the golf club. No one else wanted to help me at that point, but you did."

James was not shy with the waffle. He shoveled a spoonful of ice cream and banana waffle into his mouth. He shook his head as he chewed and swallowed.

"Happy to help, Sam. I recognized your gumption from seeing the A-list paparazzi who worked at the website in LA. Sure, they were bothering celebrities, but they have a determination, even after hitting so many roadblocks, that I knew you had, too. Consider my little tip about the golf club like an anonymous tip about which restaurant Reese Witherspoon is dining at tonight." He dug his spoon in for a second bite.

Sam laughed.

"By the way," James said, lowering his voice, "Do you know how to pronounce the name of this place? I've been living here a year, and I've actually never known."

Sam laughed again. "Hoo-gah," she said. "It's the Danish word for 'cozy,' but cozy in a way that the English word doesn't really explain."

"Ah, so 'cozy' like the feeling you get when you share

a plate of amazingly delicious food, surrounded by people you recognize, in a small town, across from a rather dashing young reporter?"

Sam nearly choked on a walnut.

"Something like that," she said, taking a quick sip of water.

Greta arrived at the table, holding out a key to Sam. A dog keychain spun on the end. It was in the shape of a greyhound, and the color, brindle.

"Since I'm assuming you're keeping your job, Pets Reporter, you can hand over your next paycheck to me as your security deposit and first month's rent," Greta said.

Sam had nearly forgotten about the apartment.

"Greta, thank you!" Sam put her spoon down and clasped her hands together.

"And dogs are allowed, in case, you know, you end up continuing to foster," Greta said. Pumpernickel stood and wagged her tail, staring at the keychain as though it were food.

"I actually talked to Dana, and I'm adopting," Sam said.

"Wow, you're like a real Birchwood resident now," James said.

"I was always a real Birchwood resident," Sam argued.

"This man's right," Greta said. "You weren't, not without a dog." Sam grabbed the keys and Greta spun and headed back to the counter.

Sam's felt a pride growing in her chest. She stared at the silver pair of keys and spinning keychain, and couldn't stop smiling. She knew she must have looked like a dope in front of James, but if he was going to ask what she thought he was going to, maybe he liked her for it.

She hadn't felt so warm and fuzzy in years. She really was a Birchwood resident, and she had the keys to prove it. Living in Hygge House with Pumpernickel suddenly sounded like something she hadn't been imaginative enough to dream of all along, but that she should have. She thought she'd be working crime in NYC someday, or at least an editor in Chicago. But now, all she wanted was to bask in the hygge of Birchwood.

"So, James," she said, meeting his ocean-blue eyes with her brown ones. "What was that you were going to ask me?"

ABOUT THE AUTHOR

Kyla Colby is a former pets reporter. *Greyhound at the Gravesite* is her first novel. Learn more at kylacolby.com.

PLEASE LEAVE A REVIEW

Enjoy this book? As an indie publisher, reviews are vital to my career.

You can help by letting me know what you think.

Please leave a review — I personally read every one.

Thank you!

—Kyla

I

PREVIEW: BOOK 2 BICHON FRISE NEAR THE BODY

BICHON FRISE
NEAR
THE BODY

Pets
Reporter
Mystery

REST
IN
PIECES

KYLA COLBY

CHAPTER ONE

S am Hodges swerved her bicycle to avoid missing a streak of brown that darted across the road. Sam's dog, Pumpernickel, whined as she skidded to a halt, too.

Sam pushed away the curly blonde hair that had fallen in her face and gasped as something else darted in front of her stopped bicycle.

"Bring! Back! My! Sock!" a man in blue overalls huffed as he chased after the brown streak. When the small burst did a quick U-turn and ran back in front of Sam's bicycle again, she recognized it as a squirrel. The small creature seemed a bit hefty in his hips, but so did the man in overalls chasing him, so they were nearly evenly matched.

The overalls man ran back across Sam again, and this time she noticed his one bare foot.

Sam walked her bicycle, Pumpernickel trotting behind, up to the dividing property line of two neighbors, the reason she was on Westward Avenue in the first place.

Sam was ready to get to the bottom of the newest pets mystery in Birchwood: the case of the chubby squirrels.

Mrs. Byrd was waiting for Sam on her front lawn, ready to launch into her spiel right away: "I'm missing several neck scarves from the clean clothes I had just taken down from the clothesline. And something has gotten into my hidden stash of bird food!" Mrs. Byrd complained as she touched her gray bouffant absently, then pointed to the notebook Sam was in the process of pulling out of her messenger bag. "Did you get that all down, dear?'"

"Yes, ma'am," answered Sam, hurrying to scribble and catch up.

As the *Birchwood Bugle*'s pets reporter, it was Sam's job to report on the overweight, fluffy-tailed rodents and how they were now suspects in a handful of burglaries. Westward residents Mrs. Byrd (pro-squirrel) and John Lowe (anti-squirrel) usually warred over Mrs. Byrd's alleged hobby of feeding Ritz crackers to the squirrels. Mrs. Byrd claimed the squirrels had nothing to do with the thefts plaguing their small suburban street. John Lowe disagreed. Vehemently.

John insisted that the increased population was behind the disappearance of a rag rug and old cloth diaper he used to dust the interior of his 1966 Mustang. He rolled up the sleeves on his maroon plaid shirt and said gruffly, "I tell you, it's those darn butterball squirrels."

Sam glanced at Lowe's property line. A cool, midwestern October breeze swept over the three of them and rustled the pristine rosebushes on Mrs. Byrd's side of the fence, and the right-angle hedges on John Lowe's side. Sam sometimes still couldn't believe *this* was her reporting duty now, after she had been a crime reporter climbing the ranks in downtown Chicago only months before.

"John's got my socks!" Mrs. Byrd said, pointing a spindly, gold-ringed finger across the fence. "He's framing them!"

John narrowed his eyes. "I'm not the one guilty of *murder*."

Mrs. Byrd shrieked. Sam lost her grip on her pen and it dropped to the ground. "Um, *what?*" Sam said, turning her head back and forth between the two angry residents.

It was only a few weeks ago that Sam helped solve a murder in Birchwood, which had nearly cost her her new job at the newspaper.

John pointed at her notebook. "Rug. Rags," he said, and after a dramatic pause, "And KOI!"

"Oh, please!" Mrs. Byrd said, waving her hand in dismissal. Sam breathed a sigh of relief. So not a *human* murder. Sam was relieved no one had lost their life but couldn't help being the smallest bit disappointed in her gut, as she was familiar with the adrenaline rush of a crime scene. She instantly felt guilty, but sometimes had trouble shaking off the career she left behind.

Mrs. Byrd continued, "Squirrels don't eat fish, and these ones are well-mannered enough to stay away from bird food, too. It's a human sneaking into my stash of bird food!"

John stepped forward toward his hedge, leaning into it. "Why would I kill my own koi babies to frame your squirrels? You're doing enough damage anyway by feeding them all those carbs! It's a death sentence!"

Sam's phone buzzed in her pocket, and Pumpernickel, her brindle greyhound who had been snoozing at her feet, jumped up and barked. The dog started hopping from foot to foot, her usual dance that indicated she was feeling impatient.

Sam gasped at the message and quickly flipped her notebook closed. "I have to get back to the office, so..."

But she was interrupted by the two neighbors, now shouting over each other and causing a scene. A dog walker across the street stopped and whipped out her cell phone to record video.

"Who cares about socks! My koi were going to be in the annual Halloween parade. Now, what am I supposed to do?"

Sam took a second to wonder just how fish would be in a parade as Mrs. Byrd continued:

"Oh, John, really. They're just fish."

John stammered and sputtered and started to turn red. "Just fish! Just fish!"

"The squirrels get plenty of exercise, and who said I'm feeding them crackers anyway!"

"I have to rethink our whole costume, now that Percy and Wendy won't be joining us!"

"Liar..."

"Murderer!"

"Enough!" Sam shouted.

Mrs. Byrd and John finally seemed to remember she was there. John stepped away from the hedge, scratching the back of his neck and muttering some apologies. Mrs.

Byrd wrapped her large, wooly cardigan more tightly around her and sighed, looking at her feet.

"I promise I'll get to the bottom of what's going on on this block," Sam said. She put her hand on her chest. "Pets reporter's promise." She cringed inwardly at the cheesiness.

"Let's just calm down for a few moments," she said in a soft voice. "Let's take a deep breath in through our noses and let it out of our mouths. In through the nose, out through the mouth." Sam couldn't believe she was actually using what she learned in dog yoga to diffuse the odd situation. She demonstrated the breathing technique while reminding herself to be a professional. John and Mrs. Byrd mimicked Sam's breathing. Even Pumpernickel, who returned to lying in the grass at Sam's feet, let out a deep breath. It was out her nose, but, well, she was a dog after all. She lowered the front of her body in a play-bow, her form of downward dog.

"I'll be in touch with both of you," Sam said, putting up the kickstand on her gray bicycle.

As she sailed off down Westward Avenue toward town, where the *Birchwood Bugle* offices were, her thoughts turned to the message and what lay ahead of her at the office.

"Mandatory all-staff meeting, ASAP," read the text message from Tom Albers, Sam's childhood friend and the recently promoted crime editor at the *Bugle*. But it was what came after that that gave Sam pause: a round, yellow-faced emoji, mouth lolling open, Xs for eyes.

A s Sam turned onto Grand Canine Way, the main boulevard in Birchwood that led into town, she made an effort not to think about what could be going on at the *Bugle*. Staff cuts were becoming a regularity in the journalism world, but certainly in this town, a pets reporter was one of the most crucial positions. Right?

Though she still felt a bit silly at times, her hometown was growing on her. Pumpernickel trotted next to Sam, and Sam was grateful for her. Most of the time, Pumpernickel was without a leash, but Sam had to be careful. Even though Birchwood was a pet's paradise, there was still a leash law, earning the culprit a $50 fine, or if Detective Jasper was feeling grouchy that day, community service. Among those pets that Sam witnessed out on a stroll that early afternoon besides the usual dogs were cats, a ferret, and a turtle (a slow stroll with Oliver the turtle and his owner John Raymond). And if an equine owner was out and about —whether he or she owned a full-size horse or a miniature one—the person had better carry a shovel along with them.

Nearly all places in Birchwood were pet friendly, including the rec center where Sam and Pumpernickel had recently graduated from dog Zumba to dog yoga two nights a week. Sam had been back in Birchwood for almost three months since a slight meltdown in Chicago, where she worked as a crime reporter for the *Chicago Times*. For the most part, she'd moved past the incident and her ex-boyfriend Steve, and embraced her new life and job in Birchwood.

Sam noticed as she rode that Birchwood was dressed to the nines with jewel-toned leaves, front stoops adorned with pumpkins and gourds, and a filter on the sun that bathed the town in golden light. Halloween was that coming weekend, and the shops along Grand Canine Way sported Halloween decorations.

"Hi, Sam!" called Clara Wilson, a young mother in town, pushing a stroller.

Sam waved back, smiling widely. Sam had once suspected Clara of murder when the town's greyhound rescue owner had been killed. But she was relieved when Clara had been proven innocent, and the two had met for coffee a few times since, especially as Clara and her husband had ended up adopting one of the greyhounds from the rescue. (It was a greyhound Clara's husband had tackled to the ground after the animals had all escaped and run amok all over town, but that was another story...)

Pumpernickel had been adopted by Sam from the same rescue. A pet wasn't something Sam had been allowed in her tiny Chicago studio, but Pumpernickel had quickly become her trusted sidekick, and they shared a small one-bedroom apartment above the local café.

Sam passed the café, Hygge House, where Greta Winters, a friend, served up delicious pastries, scrumptious coffee, and a feeling of "hygge"—or coziness in Danish.

Pumpernickel barked, and Sam turned her attention, narrowly swerving to avoid a very lifelike plastic skeleton that had found its way into the road. Though it was beautiful weather, the wind from the cornfields to the west of Birchwood was certainly picking up with autumn fervor. Sam made a mental note to tell Greta one of her decorations had escaped.

Sam locked her bike up outside the *Bugle*'s red-brick office building, and Pumpernickel followed her into the building.

The *Bugle* allowed the reporters and other staff to bring their pets to work. The *Bugle* even had its own newspaper cat—Nellie. She was a mellow brown-and-tan shorthair that Wendy Billings, the *Bugle*'s receptionist, found on the stoop of the newspaper on a cold and rainy morning three years earlier. Ignoring a persnickety scowl from Frank Martin, the paper's editor in chief and Sam's boss, Nellie became an inhabitant of the newspaper office. Even though Frank complained at Nellie's arrival, she spent her afternoons lying in his in-box, and Frank didn't seem to mind. And the worst-kept secret in the office was that Frank came into the office on the weekends to visit Nellie, although he insisted he was catching up on work.

"Sam! Have you heard?" whispered Wendy, scooting

out from behind her desk to give Pumpernickel pats once Sam stepped through the door. Wendy nervously tucked behind her ear her brunette hair that was pushed back by her usual headband.

"No, I just got a text from Tom and—"

"Hodges, is that you!" Frank yelled from inside the newsroom. It wasn't a question.

Sam raised her eyebrows at Wendy and left Pumpernickel in her care, passing through reception into the newsroom. She took a quick look around as she walked and noted that all of the news staff were there including Yolanda Oliver, the *Bugle*'s food critic. As usual, she sat with her back yardstick straight and a slight scowl on her face. Sam and Yolanda tolerated each other, although Yolanda was still having a tiny tizzy about Sam sitting in the crime section of the *Bugle*'s newsroom instead of the community news section. Frank didn't care as long as Sam stuck to animals and not crime. That wasn't quite what happened during her first week on the job, but she'd been solely focused on fur, feathers, and scales since then.

Sam had known Yolanda since she interned at the *Bugle* with Tom one adolescent summer, and Yolanda had not changed much over the years. Even her wardrobe was the same, with her plain crewneck sweater indicating the day of the week.

Since it was Monday, she wore her pale blue sweater with a color-coordinated plaid skirt. Her brown hair, long but worn in a serviceable bun at the nape of her neck, was just beginning to show a few streaks of gray. Yolanda wore the same style of glasses last popular with mature ladies in the eighties, a double strand of pearls, and sensible low pumps in black. Yolanda reminded Sam a bit of a younger Queen Elizabeth; all she was missing was a black purse and a corgi. Instead, a white bichon frise wearing a fake pink diamond collar sat primly on a miniature-sized Chesterfield sofa. As stuffy and grumpy as Yolanda was, Sam was surprised she brought Beatrice with her to work. It was so untraditional, and Yolanda was the epitome of tradition.

"Hodges!" Frank barked again, and Sam slunk into her chair next to Tom at the crime desk.

"I'm here, I'm here," she said.

Frank clapped his hands together and looked over the newsroom. The journalists in the sports section peered over their short cubicle-dividing walls (as though writing about Birchwood's few meager sports was some secret and highly serious ritual that should not be viewed by other, mere mortal, non-sportswriters). Yolanda and the movie critic swiveled their chairs around from the features section. Anne Debraun, the community news chief, stopped where she was at the copy machine as it continued to whir and chuck out papers with a whine.

"Okay!" Frank said, clapping his hands together again in what was a clear coping mechanism. Sam breathed deeply. Tom gulped audibly next to Sam. "This is our first all-staff meeting since...I'm not sure when. This is something very serious we have to talk about, as I'm sure you're aware."

Sam looked around; everyone seemed a bit on edge. Sam didn't see James Woods, the new photographer, and turned her head as subtly as possible, pretending to keep her eyes on Frank. Oh no—where was James? Sam and James had been getting to know each other better recently, and it was a relief to talk to someone who hadn't grown up in Birchwood as James had recently moved from Los Angeles, California, where he had been a paparazzo.

Frank continued, "As you know, the annual Halloween parade is coming up. Since we've been covering it, it's been one of our biggest sales of newspapers. Everyone wants to get their hands on the photo spread. James." Sam swiveled her head quickly to catch James' auburn hair and ocean-blue eyes just peeking out from the photo cave. He caught her eye and smiled. Sam smiled but looked away quickly, blushing. "We'll need to make sure you have some extra help on hand for the parade, and don't forget to take extra photos leading up to the event."

Waiting for the blow from Frank, Sam realized her nails were digging into her seat and tried to practice more dog-yoga breathing.

"I have some very bad news," Frank said, and Sam felt a collective intake of breath. "We miscounted the Halloween parade years in our paper. I can't find which year the mistake happened, but this year is *not* the twenty-fourth annual." Frank paused for dramatic effect. "This year is the *twenty-fifth* annual."

Yolanda gasped, and Sam looked around. Max Richardson looked horrified, but then she noticed he had an earbud in and was probably reacting to a sports score. Anne Debraun frowned. Was this the devastating news? Sam tried to see Tom's reaction, but he was busying himself by taking notes; sometimes it was better to use that strategy to avoid Frank's intimidating eye contact.

Frank's weathered face was more lined than ever. "First of all, this is embarrassing. We're the news. We deal in *fact*. We've gotten this wrong for years. What else could we be getting wrong? This means I'm teaming up reporters who usually don't work together so that we have twice as many eyes on our stories. We need to stay on our toes. We can't get comfortable!" He slammed one of his fists into the other. Sometimes Sam wondered whether Frank really was this much of a stereotypical hardened editor or whether he watched too many newspaper movies.

"And since it's the twenty-fifth anniversary, that milestone means we need even more coverage than usual. It's less than a week away, and we're not prepared. I'm going to need all hands on deck."

He pointed to Tom. "Albers, you're with Richardson to write about decorations this year. I'd guess they're at least double what they were last year. Why is that? Have prices dropped? The warm weather? One-upmanship from businesses and neighbors?"

Tom was still scribbling furiously. Max Richardson in sports rolled his eyes, but Frank didn't catch it.

"Hodges," Frank said next, and Sam crossed her fingers that she'd be helping James with photos. She was getting better with a camera. "You're with Oliver. See what residents are planning for their costumes."

Her face fell. Sam knew she wasn't hiding her disappointment, but when she looked over, Yolanda wasn't looking at her. The food critic's lips were pursed, and her arms folded across her cardigan. Her whole face was taut lines.

Frank continued handing out the unusual assignments and team-ups. After he was done, he retreated into his office and slammed the door.

"It's just a year off. What's he so upset about?" Sam leaned across her desk to speak to Tom. She glanced back at Frank's office, noticing Nellie pawing at the door and mewing.

"He's right, it's kind of embarrassing." Tom shrugged. "We're a newspaper. Now we're going from the twenty-third anniversary to the twenty-fifth!"

Sam frowned. It still seemed like an overreaction. What was going on with Frank? As she watched his office door, it opened quickly, and Nellie slipped in, Frank cooing to her, and then it shut harshly again.

"Okay, Albers, let's get this over with." Max Richardson stood above them, pen in his ear, bright blue-and-red Chicago Cubs jersey tucked into his jeans.

Sam excused herself and tiptoed toward Features. Yolanda was typing furiously on her computer, and Beatrice the bichon frise barked several times to announce Sam's arrival.

Sam cleared her throat, but Yolanda didn't notice. She tapped Yolanda on the shoulder, and the food critic jumped. Sam jumped in response, too.

"What!" snapped Yolanda, her purple lipstick turning into even more of a frown. "I must finish this review of the steak sandwich at Dobson's Deli. It's atrocious!"

Sam's voice came out small. She suddenly felt like a

teenage intern again around Yolanda, forgetting all her confidence as either a crime or pets reporter and Yolanda's colleague. "Well, um, we need to plan our coverage of the costumes for this year's—"

"I'm afraid I'm quite busy," Yolanda said. "I still have a bad taste in my mouth from that sandwich and an even worse one from being held up from my deadline. My prose suffers under too much stress."

Sam didn't know where to go from there. Was Yolanda flat-out refusing to work with her?

"How about we go over it tonight, then?" Sam offered. Stuck between Yolanda and Frank, she'd rather be in trouble with the person who didn't decide her employment status.

Yolanda shook her head. "No, no, no! I am reviewing the new autumn menu at Nuit Noire tonight. Privately."

"Okay, um..." Sam realized she was sweating.

Frank stuck his head out of his office. "And coverage plans are due on my desk at 9 a.m. tomorrow!" His door slammed again.

"Why is Frank acting so weird?" Sam muttered, more to herself than to Yolanda.

"I have no time to pontificate on the lives of my work colleagues, and even if I did, I find gossip distasteful. It is for those with no higher-level thinking."

Sam stood her ground. "Okay, well, we need to have this plan done by tomorrow. What do you suggest?"

"Why don't you do it?" Yolanda said, turning back to her computer and beginning to type. Beatrice jumped off her couch and barked again at Sam.

Sam sighed and tried to collect her thoughts.

"Well, if you don't contribute, Frank will notice your style isn't evident in this plan," Sam started. She looked to Yolanda for a reaction.

Yolanda had stopped typing, and Sam could see one corner of her mouth turning up just a bit into the smallest smile.

"So, we can meet after you dine at Nuit Noire."

Yolanda turned and gasped, horrified. "No!" she said. Beatrice looked up to her owner, cocking her head to the side in confusion, her diamond-encrusted collar sparkling. "I am in bed by 9 p.m. sharp! I haven't been out later than that in twenty years." She shook her head and sighed loudly. "Fine. If you must, you may also attend Nuit Noire."

Sam internally jumped for joy.

Yolanda held her index finger up. "But no meddling!"

Sam shrugged as innocently as she could. What could possibly cause her to meddle?

CHAPTER THREE

A t five to seven that evening, Sam walked the couple of blocks to Nuit Noire from the *Bugle* offices. Yolanda had gone home promptly at 5 p.m. (schedules were her thing, it seemed), but Sam stayed late, prepping what she could for the costume coverage and putting out a few phone

calls to squirrel experts at the major Illinois universities for her Westwood Avenue story.

As Sam walked, she peered into the shops, the inside lights coming on in anticipation of the looming sunset in twenty minutes. Birchwood, although modern, with high-speed internet access and even a food delivery service, still retained many characteristics of a small town and different era when it was safe for young women to be out walking as the sun set. Junior high boys, and the occasional girl, still delivered the *Bugle* before the sun was up. Although bike helmets were the norm, the streetlights still indicated when it was time for youth to be home. Or, at least, reminded them to pocket their smartphones and head home from Memorial Park.

Yes, ma'am and *no, ma'am* were still heard sometimes, along with the masculine equivalents. Doors were held open, and Birchwood even had a dairy that delivered milk and cream to square metal boxes on residents' porches. But modernity was creeping into town. The pants-less ordered dinner through Alexa, received Chicago traffic from Siri, and then bought commuter train tickets on their smartphones for the ease of going into work in the Windy City. Sam's mom, always a proper woman, began to wear white after Labor Day. Birchwood now even had a vegan café/health-food store run by Rainbow Love, a wannabe hippie who was born two decades after the Summer of Love. Rainbow, also known as Mary Jane Johnson, was a bit off her rocker and believed that pets were the actual parents and humans were the pets. The judge denied Rainbow's request to have her dalmatian and cross-eyed Siamese cat declared as her adoptive parents.

The decorative orange Halloween streetlights were on, and Sam's walk was pleasant. She passed a few people on their evening walk with their dogs, and Pumpernickel stopped to greet the canines. She touched noses with a Chihuahua and sniffed the opposite end of a bull mastiff. Some stopped and chitchatted with Sam about the upcoming annual Halloween parade, which was mostly a pets parade. Everyone wanted to know what costumes others would be wearing but didn't want to reveal their own ideas. Some owners made their own costumes, but more went to Danielle's Everyday Dog

Wear, where Danielle swore she would keep everyone's secrets.

"And what will Pumpernickel be wearing?" asked a young man with a Rottweiler who Sam didn't recognize.

"Promise you won't tell anyone?" Sam said.

"On my honor," he replied.

"I ordered a doggy chef's uniform complete with a chef's toque." Pumpernickel raised her head and whined at Sam, clearly unhappy with having to wear a tall, difficult-to-balance hat.

The man laughed. "And her cuisine specialty? Classic French? Asian fusion? American nouveau?"

Sam laughed as she answered, "Hot dogs."

Sam arrived at Nuit Noire and took in the ornately carved front doors with etched windows. Sam remembered so many birthday celebrations at the diner that used to stand in its place that she felt a bit awkward entering the restaurant. The restaurant was only a few years old.

"Bienvenue à Nuit Noire," a put-on French accent greeted Sam as she pushed open the front door, and Pumpernickel trotted inside. Behind a light wood, rustic maître d' stand stood a tall man with a clean but stubbled beard and piercing green eyes.

"Um, hmm, oh, of course, merci!" Sam said, not believing she could forget even the French word for thank you after five years of study of the language.

"Ms. Oliver said I should look out for a young woman who would be joining her for the special tasting of the autumn menu. I look forward to hearing your thoughts." The man's accent was actually British.

Sam blushed. She hadn't thought she'd be eating, too, only joining Yolanda at her table. "The chef didn't have to make another course for me!"

The man behind the maître d' stand waved his hand. "No trouble at all. If you don't mind," he said, gesturing to the back kitchen.

"No, not at all," Sam said. The man pointed to a table in the center of the other tables, set for two.

Sam meandered to the table with Pumpernickel and looked around the walls. She tried but couldn't remember what the diner had looked like. The furniture now was a collection of rustic pieces painted cream, periwinkle, and pale yellow. There were small tables scattered about and two antique open china hutches that held mismatched plates, bowls, and cups. In the corner, a single place setting was at a small table, the only other table with dishes on it.

Just then Yolanda came into the dining area from a hallway, wiping her hands. Sam guessed she had come from the bathroom. Beatrice trotted behind her and barked again at Sam.

"Late, I see," Yolanda greeted Sam. Pumpernickel rose to say hello to Yolanda, but Yolanda walked right past her. Beatrice did, too.

Sam did a few deep dog-yoga breaths. She hoped to enjoy the nice dinner, despite Yolanda's presence.

Yolanda settled herself into her chair and Sam did the same.

"Where is everyone?" Yolanda asked, straightening her cardigan. "The service here, tut tut."

"The maître d' welcomed me but went back into the kitchen."

Yolanda's mouth fell open, and she picked up the sparkling water in front of her. "Maître d'! Maître d'. Oh my." She sipped. "Don't you recognize one of the most famous chefs in the world when you see him?"

Sam was not good with faces, but something tickled the back of her brain.

Yolanda looked on with disdain. "Hugh Spen-cer-And-er-son," she said, saying it slowly as though Sam were a child learning her first words.

"Oh yeah..." Sam said, not sure she could place the name she recognized as that of a celebrity chef (there were so many these days, weren't there?) but just then, Hugh reappeared from the kitchen, his hands behind his back.

"And now, my ladies," Hugh said.

Sam held out her hand, prepared to be handed the menu for the evening. But Hugh whipped his hands out from behind his back not to reveal menus, but two black strips of fabric. He placed one into Sam's hand, but Yolanda's hands remained primly folded in front of her.

"What sort of gimmick is this, Hugh?" Yolanda said skeptically.

"A special Halloween menu!" he said, his perfectly straight white, gleaming Hollywood teeth glistening in the dimly lit restaurant. "I can't believe I haven't used it in this restaurant before, but just imagine!" He spread his hands before him, his eyes getting a faraway glint in them. "Diners, blindfolded! The textures, the tastes like they've never experienced them before! Without their eyes to bias them, each molecule on the tongue, each waft into the nose, is pure, unadulterated, heightened, even!" He beamed.

Sam eagerly sat higher in her chair, excited. She'd never heard of a dining-in-the-dark restaurant before. Yolanda, predictably, rolled her eyes but outstretched her hand to take the blindfold. Hugh winked at Sam as Yolanda took it, and Sam couldn't help but smile shyly back at the handsome chef.

"Oh, and I almost forgot!" he said, bringing out two more, smaller blindfolds. He gently tied them around Pumpernickel and Beatrice's snouts, so that the fabric just covered their noses. "Think of how heightened a dog's sense of taste will be without his sense of smell! I have a special meal for you two, as well." He knelt down and patted the dogs, who were already trying to knock the smell-blindfolds off with their paws.

Hugh stood. "Blindfolds on, ladies, l'aperitif shall be arriving shortly." Hugh waited until Sam and Yolanda had both put their blindfolds on.

Hugh was right, Sam thought. As soon as her blindfold was on, she felt all her other senses were heightened. She heard Hugh's footsteps recede and heard his light humming as he went back to the kitchen. Pumpernickel whined next to Sam, and she reached out, a wet nose underneath a cloth finding her fingers. "It's okay, Pump," Sam said. Sam could hear Yolanda breathing softly, and she thought even the critic's natural breathing rhythm had a twinge of annoyance to it.

She heard a faint buzzing of the dim lights in the

restaurant, and the howl of wind outside as the overnight chill picked up this late into October.

Hugh's footsteps came back, and something was set down on the table in front of Sam.

"A small spoon will be on your right. Not traditional place settings, but rearranged for the ease of the...well, situation," Hugh said.

Sam reached for her spoon, fumbling around on the table until she found the metal.

"And what is this dish?" asked Yolanda.

"Ah you see, that's the beauty of this menu! You won't know until the end, when I'll reveal each course to you and show you a picture of what you've eaten."

Yolanda tsk'd, but Sam thought she could hear a bit of a smile in the food critic's voice.

"Bon appétit," Hugh said, and his footsteps receded once again.

Sam put her spoon in front of her, hitting the table. She tried again and clinked a dish. She then found something soft and brought her spoon up to her mouth.

The flavors exploded in her mouth: salty, crisp, a squishy texture. She hadn't the slightest clue what she was eating.

"How is it, Yolanda?" Sam asked. Yolanda only tutted in reply. "Yolanda, I was thinking for our pet costume coverage, we could shadow Danielle from her Everyday Dog Wear store..." Sam started, but Yolanda cut her off.

"Please, I need to concentrate! I can't even see what I'm eating."

Sam fell silent, concentrating on trying to guess her

food. She put her spoon in another spot on the plate, and it came away with something crunchy, salty, and nutty.

Sam heard a rustling behind her a short while later. Must be Hugh, she thought. But then his footsteps came again from her right, where the kitchen was.

"And now, the hors d'oeuvres," he said. "Be careful, it might be a bit hot. A new spoon is on your right."

Sam picked up the new spoon, and it sank into a pool of liquid in front of her. She felt a sudden chill break over her as she brought her spoon to her mouth. But suddenly, the hot liquid seemed to spread down Sam's throat, across her chest, into her belly. The contrast of the cool air and warm soup was divine. She pulled her sweater around her, feeling goose bumps on her arms. Sam heard a rustling sound, like Beatrice was digging in her or Yolanda's bag.

"Pumpkin! How original for fall!" Yolanda said sarcastically, and Pumpernickel whined and jumped up with her two front paws on Sam's lap. Sam could feel the skinny legs of her greyhound and recognized her cry.

"She said *pumpkin*, not Pumpernickel," Sam said. Sam took another bite of the soup, and it was pumpkin, but with a distinctly herby flavor, too.

Sam and Yolanda sat in silence, and Sam thought her experience of time had been heightened, too. But she was set off-balance. Without her ability to see, she wasn't sure how quickly the time was passing. How long had she and Yolanda been in the restaurant? Twenty minutes? Ten? She soon scraped the bottom of her soup bowl and could hear Yolanda finishing hers up, too.

Pumpernickel whined again. "I'm sure Hugh is bringing your dish soon, Pump," Sam said.

A few more minutes (Sam guessed) passed in silence.

"Oh, really, now," Yolanda said. "This is getting ridiculous! How long could it take someone to eat soup?"

There was a crash from the kitchen, and Sam froze. Beatrice started barking, and it sounded like she was far away. Sam had the instinct to rip off her blindfold but didn't. She didn't want to ruin Hugh's meticulously crafted dining experience, even if he had dropped a dish in the kitchen. He was a career chef; it probably wasn't the first accident he'd had.

"I'm going back there," Yolanda said.

"Let's wait," Sam said. She liked Hugh; she didn't want Yolanda to give him an even worse review than she was sure the food critic was already writing in her head. "I'm sure he's just a bit behind schedule. Give him another minute."

Sam heard Yolanda's chair scrape backward. "Yolanda," Sam said.

"I'm not taking my blindfold off," she snapped. "Hugh? Hugh!"

Sam heard Yolanda stepping toward the kitchen slowly and carefully. And then *crack!*

"Arghhh!" Yolanda yelped. "My toe! Oh, this is ridiculous."

The next thing Sam heard was Yolanda screaming. Sam jumped up and ripped off her blindfold. She rushed into the kitchen, where she found a horrible scene.

Yolanda's hands were on each side of her face like *The Scream* painting, her mouth open in horror at the body of Hugh Spencer-Anderson, sprawled on the floor. The huge soup pan was overturned, and the chef was covered in the orange liquid.

Beatrice stood next to him, her pristine white fur also dripping with soup. The bichon frise's little pink tongue wound around and around her nose to lick it off.

Sam didn't even think to try her dog-yoga breathing as a sense of panic began rising in her chest.

To keep reading, buy Bichon Frise Near the Body here.

CONTINUE THE SERIES

Buy book 2 in the Pets Reporter cozy mystery series

Bichon Frise Near the Body

Buy on Amazon now!

To be the first to know about the launch of *Book 3: Pot-Bellied Pig in Peril*, join my author mailing list at kylacolby.com